D0005524

DATE DUE			

Two Lies and a SPY

KAT CARLTON

SIMON & SCHUSTER BFYR

New York London Toronto Sydney New Delhi

SIMON & SCHUSTER BFYR

An imprint of Simon & Schuster Children's Publishing Division
1230 Avenue of the Americas, New York, New York 10020

This book is a work of fiction. Any references to historical events, real people,
or real places are used fictitiously. Other names, characters, places, and events
are products of the author's imagination, and any resemblance to actual events
or places or persons, living or dead, is entirely coincidental.

SIMON & SCHUSTER BFYR is a trademark of Simon & Schuster, Inc.
For information about special discounts for bulk purchases, please contact Simon & Schuster
Special Sales at 1-866-506-1949 or business@simonandschuster.com.
The Simon & Schuster Speakers Bureau can bring authors to your live event.
For more information or to book an event, contact the Simon & Schuster Speakers Bureau
at 1-866-248-3049 or visit our website at www.simonspeakers.com.
Book design by Krista Vossen
Jacket photograph of girl and boys copyright © 2013 by
Michael Frost; photograph of car and tunnel copyright © 2013 by
Adrian Assalve/Vetta/Getty Images; photograph of
Capitol building copyright © 2013 by Jodi Jacobson/E+/Getty Images
The text for this book is set in Berling LT Std.
Manufactured in the United States of America
2 4 6 8 10 9 7 5 3
Library of Congress Cataloging-in-Publication Data
Carlton, Kat.
Two lies and a spy / Kat Carlton.— First edition.
pages cm
Summary: Sixteen-year-old Kari juggles saving her spy parents while impressing the guy she
has been in love with forever.
ISBN 978-1-4424-8172-5 (hardcover : alk. paper)
ISBN 978-1-4424-8174-9 (eBook)
[1. Spies—Fiction. 2. Parents—Fiction. 3. Brothers and sisters—Fiction. 4. Love—Fiction.]
I. Title.
PZ7.C216852Tw 2013
[Fic]—dc23
2013006449

Stories could not exist without an enthusiastic audience to receive them, so this novel is dedicated, with thanks, to young readers everywhere. May books continue to fuel your imagination, your dreams, and your sense of adventure!

ACKNOWLEDGMENTS

With special thanks to Dani Young, covert creative operative and editor extraordinaire.

A big thanks is also due to Sophia Alichos, the best teen "beta reader" anyone could hope for! And to Aleka Nakis. Your feedback was greatly appreciated. Finally, thanks to Greg H., for shedding some light on the scary and fascinating world of computer hacking.

Chapter One

Can u pick up milk on ur way home?

It's not the kind of text that would make most people climb out of a bathroom window. It comes across as pretty harmless, right? But it's not, trust me. And I'm not most people.

I'm Kari Andrews, and I'm a junior here at the ivy-covered, lushly landscaped, Kennedy Preparatory School in Washington, DC. Yeah, I've definitely looked more dignified than I do right now as I dangle half out of the ladies' room window. I'm scrambling for a hand-hold between the climbing ivy and the old red brick and mortar that surrounds the window so I can pull myself up and out, then drop the four and a half feet to the grass below.

I hit the ground running.

I'm not playing hooky—this is a Code Black emergency.

Twenty minutes ago

I'm sitting in art class, spinning the sterling silver charm that I got in the mail yesterday from my parents. They travel a lot, so they send little gifts to my brother Charlie and me, just to let us know that they're thinking about us.

I'm trying to get excited about painting a still life in the style of an old Dutch master. Van Eyck or Holbein or Rembrandt—one of those sixteenth-century men in tights with a long droopy nose and a silly hat sporting a peacock feather.

The still life involves a green velvet drape under a porcelain bowl of fruit. Next to the bowl sits a creepy antique doll with blond corkscrew curls. I block out some shapes on my paper with pencil and then mix the green paint for the drape, but I am unsure exactly where to start with the composition. Drapery's tough, and I'm not much of an artist.

I'm spinning my charm, which is Romania's Bran Castle, on the long paint-and-clay-spattered table. Dracula's legendary home hits an old blob of dried paste, then jumps and skitters right into my little lake of green. Go figure—I should have taken the time to attach it to my bracelet with the others.

My best friend Larita, who has the same art period, sees, snorts, and tries not to laugh. I just fish the charm out of the puddle of green and clean it off with a paper towel, then I stick it in my pocket and go back to staring at the still life. The doll has big brown eyes and wears a disdainful expression on her sculpted plastic lips that reminds me exactly of the way Lacey Carson looks when she bothers to notice me.

I pull out my cell phone to text Rita about the resemblance of the doll to Lacey, but I never get the chance. The "get milk" message from my dad pops up, and I know I have to clear out fast. In our family that milk message doesn't mean what you think it means. It's code for a true emergency.

I get up from my stool and head for the door. Mr. Aldrich barely glances at me, he's so laid-back. Good thing this text came right now and not during algebra, because it would've been a lot harder to get away from Colonel Davenport. (We call him Colon D because he's so anal—but that's another topic.)

I slide out the door and into Kennedy Prep's blue-tiled hallway. Because Kale, my other best friend, is due to pick me up for a martial arts class after school, I quickly text him not to come and not to worry if I'm out of contact for a while.

Then I run to Rita's locker. The first rule in case of an emergency like this one is to ditch my phone, with its handy GPS chip. Rita will know how to get in touch with me when she finds it.

I'm happy that my hands don't shake at all as I turn the dial left to 17, right to 43, and then left again to 26. I slide the phone under Rita's left gym shoe, at the bottom of the locker, and swipe a handful of her Peanut M&M's. After all, a girl needs protein when she's on the run.

I pop a few into my mouth, then crunch down. So my teeth are nice and brown and gooey when two pairs of feet appear on the other side of the locker door, one in highly polished Italian loafers and the other in scuffed boat shoes. I know those feet.

I look up and meet the amused gazes of Evan Kincaid, International Jerk of Mystery, and Luke Carson, American Hottie—and twin brother of Doll-Face Lacey.

Luke, who's Abercrombie and Fitch all the way, is the best-looking guy in all of Kennedy Prep, and he's got an easygoing personality that made him a shoo-in for junior class president.

Luke's got muscular runner's legs to die for—not that I can see them right now under his khakis. His broad chest and buff arms hold my attention just fine, thanks. He's blond like Lacey and tan from all the time he spends outdoors on the track team. He has the same big brown eyes as his sister, but his are warm and intelligent as opposed to vacuous and ringed by mascara.

But it's Luke's smile that makes him irresistible. He gets these dimples at the corners of his mouth that should be illegal, and he has a way of making a girl feel that she's the only person in the world who matters to him. I'm not sure how he does it—or if he's even aware of it—but I am a slave to those dimples.

"And what have we here? An assassin or a thief?" The question distracts me. It's delivered in a lazy, British public school drawl, the voice deeper than it has a right to be—and at the same time silky.

Evan Kincaid appeared out of nowhere this fall. Supposedly he's from London, and there's a rumor that his parents work for the British Embassy, but Rita says that's not true. He's taller than Luke, about six feet, and a little broader.

Too broad, if you ask me. He probably oils up and pumps iron in a gym full of mirrors. He's got smoky-gray eyes that sometimes go blue, like right now. His light brown hair always looks windswept but perfect, and even though we have to wear uniforms at Kennedy Prep, his shirts are tailored, not store-bought like everyone else's. He gets a ten out of ten for style from Fashionista Rita.

Evan may look as if he stepped out of GQ, but it's Luke who does funny things to me. I get discombobulated around him and my knees turn to rubber. I also do dumb things—like forget I have M&M's in my mouth as I greet him with a big smile.

"Hi, Luke." I clap my hand over my mouth, mortified.

Evan guffaws. "Seen a dentist lately, love?"

Even Luke, who's a really nice guy, struggles to keep a straight face.

I can't speak for the horror of the situation. So naturally, Evan does for me.

"She's definitely an assassin," he says to Luke. "Because if looks could kill, I'd be in rigor mortis by now."

"Nope." Luke allows himself a smile. His eyes run slowly down my body as if by instinct, but then he averts them, instead of ogling. Not that I have much to ogle. "She's a thief. Because this isn't her locker—it's Rita's. And those are probably Rita's M&M's. Am I right?"

My face has already flash fried. Now my neck does too—and the rest of me—under Luke's gaze. I want to tell Evan that I want to kill him, all right. But slowly. Taking hours to do it. So rigor mortis? It's a long way off.

But I can't say that in front of Luke. I swallow the M&M's. Struggle for some dignity. And find my voice. "I was starving, and Rita said I could have some. What are you guys doing out of class?"

"Doc's appointment," Luke says easily.

I flick a disinterested glance toward Evan, along with a raised eyebrow.

"Just bored." He yawned. "Colon D's class. No need to solve for X. It's on the stick that's up his—"

"How did you get past him?" Against my will, I'm impressed.

"Got my ways and means, love."

"I'm not your *love*." No mystery why I feel the need to assert this in front of Luke.

Evan flashes too-white teeth at me. "Pity, that."

I roll my eyes. Mature, no—but it relieves my feelings somewhat.

"So," Evan inquires, "ditching school yourself, are you?"

I shoot a glance at Luke, who's kind of a Boy Scout. "No, of course not." I really need to get out of Dodge, but I can't risk Evan trying to accompany me. How to handle this?

How would my mom handle it? Chic, petite, elegant . . . never a dark hair out of place, she can make any man squirm at a glance—and this includes my dad. I hear her voice in my head, dishing out one of her many pieces of invaluable advice. *Men will rarely follow a woman into the bathroom, darling.*

"I'm not playing hooky . . . just going to the ladies' room."

Luke looks at his watch, then shifts his weight from one foot to the other. "Well. I've got to run—don't want to be late. See you."

"'Kay," I squeak, still doing my best to scrape chocolate and nut particles off my teeth with my tongue.

Evan seems to know exactly what I'm doing. And because he's watching, I can't even check out Luke's truly fine rear end as he walks away. I slam Rita's locker door and scuttle like a cockroach, not a lady, in the other direction.

"Always delightful to see you," Evan calls after me.

I ignore him and refuse to let him bother me.

Adrenaline beats in a tiny, staccato pulse under my jaw. Are my parents okay?

Of *course* they're *fine*. They've been in and out of tough situations in the past. This alarm won't be any different—it probably just means that we'll have to go through the hassle of revamping all our security.

I push open the door of the girls' bathroom and wrinkle my nose at the weird, fake cherry smell of the disinfectant in there. A quick glance in the mirror reveals that my hair is still long, dark, and kind of messy; my face is your average face with two brown eyes, a nose, and a mouth. Aunt Sophie is always hassling me to wear some makeup—but the stuff mystifies me. On the few occasions that I've experimented with it, I have ended up making myself look like either a clown or a hooker.

Too bad there's not a whole lot to do in a girls'

bathroom if you're not big on primping. I don't even need to pee. A speck of green paint under my thumbnail gives me an excuse to wash my hands, but that doesn't take up much time.

I check my watch: Two minutes have gone by. I decide to open the door a crack and see if Evan is still loitering in the hallway.

Unfortunately, he is, for some unknown and completely annoying reason. *Go away!* I mouth.

Oblivious, he continues to text something on his phone.

I check my watch again. How to get out of here? I need to go meet my little brother Charlie, stat.

Charlie, who is only seven, is already a fifth grader at James Madison Academy, because he's basically a genius and has skipped three grades. I worry sometimes that he's *too* smart. It would do him good to get out and play with other kids more—but he's shy, and they tend to think that he's a little odd. How many seven-year-olds are fluent in four languages? Can quote Nietzsche and Schopenhauer? And write computer code in Java, C++ and PHP?

Yeah, he's a walking brain.

Evan shows no sign of moving anytime soon, so I start looking for a way around him—and hone in on the small, frosted-glass windows over the two sinks in the girls' bathroom.

One of them is sealed shut, but I manage to get the other one open. I vault up onto the sink and wriggle my head and shoulders through the tight rectangle. Sometimes being small for my age is a curse, but right now it's a beautiful thing. And unlike Lacey, I have no long pink nails to break as I scrabble for gaps in the mortar. I get my right arm all the way out and cling to the window frame like a monkey with my left one. I find a good handhold among the bricks and shimmy out to my knees, my butt in the air and my plaid uniform skirt flapping. Anyone standing around outside would get a great visual of my blue polka-dotted panties, but no one's there, thank God.

The cold metal of the window casing presses against my bare thighs and makes me shiver. Immodestly I work one leg free of the window until I'm straddling it. The chilly, early October air wafts over my skin as I dangle by one leg from that freakin' window, using my other foot to brace against the bricks outside. I stick my arm back through and grab my backpack off the sink, then drop it into a pile of leaves below me. I scrape my second knee through the frame, hang from the pediment like an orangutan for a moment, and then drop to the grass. I run from the grounds toward the road that will take me southeast to Wisconsin Avenue and the Metro stop there.

Hang on, Charlie. I'm coming for you.

Chapter Two

My little brother sits by himself on a bench in Georgetown Playground, located between Thirty-third and Thirty-fourth Streets just a bit west of Wisconsin. He's wearing the James Madison uniform of khakis, white button-down, and blue blazer. Wisps of his blond hair are askew, and his tortoise-shell glasses have slipped half an inch down his nose. He looks like a miniature banker on casual Friday. I hide a smile when I see that he is actually scanning an old copy of *Roget's International Thesaurus*.

"Hey, kiddo. Doing a little light reading?"

"Misrepresent," says Charlie, nodding. "Belie, give a wrong idea, put in a false light, pervert, distort, garble, twist, warp, wrench, slant"—he takes a breath—"twist the meaning of, color, miscolor . . . falsify, misteach, disguise, camouflage"—he takes another breath—"misstate, misreport, misquote, overstate, exaggerate, overdraw, understate, travesty, parody, caricature, burlesque."

I have to laugh. "And hello to you, too."

He grins, and I ruffle his hair.

Then Charlie's grin fades. "Dad sent me a text. *'Don't forget your inhaler.'* Code Black."

I nod. "Yup. So we wait here for an hour until Mom and Dad show up."

Charlie nods, shoves his glasses back up his nose, then chews on his lip. "What do you think happened?"

"I don't know, Charlie Brown." I use my most unconcerned voice, because I don't want my brother to stress out. He worries a lot. But he doesn't worry about the things that normal seven-year-olds do: a broken iPod, or missing an episode of *SpongeBob SquarePants*, or how he did on a spelling test.

No, Charlie is concerned about the Texas-size mass of floating garbage in the ocean and how it's getting bigger, probably leaking toxins into the water and poisoning the fish. He wants to know why nothing is being done about it. He wants to know where the US will put its garbage after the ocean is full—will rockets take it to outer space and toss it on Mars?

And don't get him started on global warming.

"I'm not Charlie Brown," he says now. "I'm Charlie Andrews."

I stick out my hand, the charms on my bracelet tinkling. "Nice to meet you."

He peers at me through his glasses, giving me his owl look. "And stop trying to distract me from the problem at hand. That is a very transparent tactic."

I have to laugh again. He sounds exactly like Mom. How many times has she said that over the years, as we've tried to manipulate her into buying something we want, or wheedle our way out of a jam?

That is a very transparent tactic, Karina.

"Busted," I admit.

He waggles his index finger at me.

"So do you want to play on the swings?"

"Not so much," he says dryly. "I don't like sitting on pigeon poop."

I try to think of something to do to pass the time, besides pacing back and forth in front of him until I've dug a trench.

"I could read aloud some more of *Roget's*," he offers. "The next word is five hundred seventy-four: 'art'. It's pretty cool. Some guy named J. F. Millet says it's 'a treating of the commonplace with the sublime,' but I have to look up 'sublime' because I'm not sure exactly what that means."

I shake my head. My little brother is amazing. Strange, but truly impressive.

"Do *you* know what it means? Sublime?"

"Um . . . I think it means sort of, I don't know—noble? Grand?"

"Oh. I guess that makes sense."

I look at my watch. Where are Mom and Dad?

"You don't want me to read *Roget's* aloud, do you?" Charlie inquires.

I shake my head, even though I should probably encourage him to learn. But the problem is that Charlie wants to learn everything, all the time. He needs to go play ball or catch bugs or even watch cartoons, like a normal child. He needs to play with other kids, not explore the theory of relativity. Lately he's even studying German—as if he doesn't already speak Russian, French, and Spanish! The kid puts me to shame. I suck at languages.

Martial arts are my thing. "Want me to teach you some karate moves?"

Charlie yawns.

Guess not.

"So, tell me about your day," I prompt him. "What did you study?"

He launches into a half-hour history lesson about the coal mining industry in West Virginia.

I ask him a few questions before I frown. "Wait— you're learning about this in fifth grade?"

Well, no. Not exactly. But Charlie, as usual, got bored with the real lesson and snuck an encyclopedia behind his textbook.

I would laugh, but I'm used to these stories.

Then Charlie's expression changes from professorial to puzzled. "Hey, isn't that Mitch over there?"

I look over my shoulder. Sure enough, a friend of our parents is crossing the park, another guy in a gray suit following him.

Now I'm worried. Really worried. Where are Mom and Dad? And why is Mitch here?

"Hey, kiddo," I say. "Do me a favor? Go over to where all those nannies are, on the playground."

"Why?"

"It's just a tactical move, Charlie. We're supposed to meet Mom and Dad, not Mitch—and I just want to be careful. Mitch is nowhere in our playbook."

"Okay." Charlie grabs his backpack and the copy of *Roget's* and heads off. I stand up and walk toward Mitch and Gray Suit Man.

Mitch is a stocky guy in dress slacks and an open-necked shirt. He's got short brown hair that's going gray at the temples and these sort of silvery-gray eyes. He'd look like a normal businessman, except that he's clearly ex-military. It's in his walk, the way he holds himself.

"Hi, Kari!" he calls in hearty tones. A little too hearty.

Here's the thing—Mitch is one of those guys that I've always been indifferent to. He's been at the house for dinner before, and maybe a couple of parties. A barbecue. He's not exactly nice, but he's not not-nice, either. He's just there: a department-store dummy of a man.

Mitch gives me a professional grin. "Karina, glad you're here. Your mom and dad asked me to swing by and pick you two up."

"Where are they?" I ask. My nose is starting to itch. I have this really weird thing—when someone is lying to me and I know it, my nose tickles. Sounds crazy, but it's true.

"They're safe, don't worry." He nods reassuringly.

I feel like I'm going to sneeze. "Um, who's this?" I look at Gray Suit Man.

"Oh, this is . . . Gary. Gary Simons. He works at the Agency with us."

"Hello, Karina. Nice to meet you." Simons has a gravelly smoker's voice, and his hair is as gray as his suit. His skin is grayish too. And he's got small, weasel eyes with big pouches of skin under them.

It takes me two point five seconds to decide that I do not like this guy. "Yeah," I say, with just the hint of a polite smile. "Nice to meet you, too." I take an involuntary step back from him and turn to Mitch. "So what's the password?"

Mitch blinks. "Ah. To be honest, there wasn't time for Cal and Irene to even think about that. We had to rush them to a safe house."

I sneeze.

"Gesundheit," Mitch says, still in that gung ho, overly familiar tone.

"Thanks." Out of the corner of my eye, I see Gary Simons take two quick steps toward me, as if he's going to grab me.

I pivot and launch myself at Mitch, driving my right shoulder into his stomach.

Mitch, caught off guard, doubles over. His skull collides with Simons. I have a split second to get away.

I sprint.

But ex-military Mitch recovers fast and grips my arm in a vise. I can't plow my elbow into his gut because he's got it immobilized. With another pivot I face him and slam my heel toward his groin. Mitch isn't stupid—he knows better than to let that blow connect.

He twists and sidesteps, but I've knocked him off-balance. He's going down.

He can either let go of me and brace for impact, or he can hang on to me and take me down with him.

Bad for me that he chooses option two.

Think, Kari. Think.

He hits the dirt, and I land on top of him. Gray Gary reaches for me again.

I head-butt Mitch right in the face and hear his nose crunch. I'm sorry to say that it's a satisfying sound. My good buddy Mitch forgets to compliment my technique.

"Bitch!" he screams.

Simons grabs me around the middle and pulls me off his friend. He's strong, but that midsection of his is soft as he drags me backward. I throw myself forward and then drive back with my heel, aiming for his knee. No luck.

So I smash both elbows into his squishy middle: one, two. He gasps, wheezes.

The guy has breath like a camel.

I get him in the groin with my hip bone, and, with a moan, he lets go of me.

That's when I strike out and connect my right foot with his left knee. He goes down into the dirt and howls like a strangled coyote—I'm pretty sure I've shattered his kneecap.

Run, Kari! Run!

I cannot let these jerks take me. If they get me, then Charlie is an easy target.

I sprint toward the playground area.

But I don't get too far.

Because Mitch, whose legs are longer than mine, catches up to me within four strides. This time he grabs both of my arms and twists them behind my back, which really hurts. Charlie and his thesaurus might call it excruciating.

These apes are *not* getting Charlie. So, since fighting like a man hasn't worked, I scream like a girl. I scream so loud that I'm sure my throat and lungs will explode. "Kidnapper! *Kidnapper!* Help me!"

A couple dozen nannies turn in our direction—and a lot of them have cell phones pressed to their ears.

I have Mitch's blood all over my uniform, since his nose gushed like a geyser when I head-butted him. The nannies can tell that I'm not crying wolf. In fact, one of them steps forward and yells, "I'm calling the cops!"

Mitch curses again—this time it's long and colorful. But he has to let me go. He's got no choice. He releases my arms and shoves me away from him.

I don't wait for him to change his mind. I jerk my thumb at Charlie, and we both take off running for the west edge of the park. Trees and grass are a green blur; the wind tears at my hair; adrenaline still pounds through my veins.

When Charlie and I intersect, I reach for his hand and tow him out of the park, heading northwest. He is visibly upset. "Why did Mitch grab you? How come you've got blood on your shirt? Who is that other guy?"

Charlie's not crying, but he is trembling and his lower lip quivers.

"Kiddo, I don't know what's going on, but I'm fine. And this is not my blood—it's Mitch's. I think I broke his nose."

"You did?"

"Yeah."

Charlie thinks about that as we hustle along. "Cool."

"Well, not so much . . . but he did try to grab me first. They both did. So what I did was self-defense."

"When all else fails, resort to violence," Charlie says solemnly. "Like Dad says."

My dad is just being sarcastic, and the "violence" is usually done to an inanimate object that he's trying to fix. "Yeah, but only when all else fails. Okay?"

He nods.

We emerge on Thirty-fourth Street and keep moving north, toward Q Street and the closest Metro station. Unfortunately, it's over a mile away and we attract attention, because my shirt is bloody.

An old lady just stares at us. A businessman frowns but says nothing. A man in fatigues calls out, "Are you two all right? Do you need help?"

"Oh, no thanks," I tell him. "It's actually ketchup." I laugh, convincingly, I hope. After all, he can't know that my voice is an octave higher than it usually is. "My little brother was trying to open two packets at once for his French fries, and they squirted all over me." I roll my eyes and throw up my hands. "What can you do?"

Charlie says nothing, which is probably good.

The guy in fatigues looks at me funny, and I'm pretty sure he knows it's not ketchup that's on my shirt. But then he just shrugs and goes on his way.

My knees are shaking and I've got to lose this shirt, like, yesterday. But we're almost to our destination, which is Dupont Circle, so I mop at my face with my shirtsleeve, twist my messy hair into a knot, and take off my backpack, holding it in front of me as we walk. I look at my watch. We're half an hour early to this checkpoint. I really hope Mom and Dad make it this time. But the Mitch-and-Gary show back there puts a bad feeling in the pit of my stomach.

What's going on? How would they have known about our meeting points in case of a Code Black? That's family-only knowledge. So did they get the information from Mom and Dad? And if so, then why did they try to force us to go with them? Have they *done* something to our parents?

"Why do you think Mom and Dad didn't come?" Charlie asks.

"They probably just got held up somewhere," I say breezily.

As we get on the Metro and head southeast across town, I really, really hope that's true.

Chapter Three

Union Station is a huge, classical white building—really more than one building. It's not only a train station, it's also a mall with tons of shops and restaurants and access to the Metro. I've loved it ever since I was a kid. It's been around forever, but in the eighties they did a massive renovation and gave the grand old lady a lot of cosmetic surgery. She really struts her stuff now.

Before we duck inside, I do a quick scan of the crowd around us. I know Mitch and Gary weren't on our Metro train, but it bothers me that they knew where to meet us at the Georgetown Playground. Do they know that my parents have a locker here, too? Are they aware of the entire Andrews family backup plan?

The lockers at Union Station are near Gate A on the Amtrak Concourse, so we head over there. I know the combination by heart and have since before I was

Charlie's age—I just never seriously thought we'd have to do more than a drill.

I have the door open with a few twists of the lock—31-61-91—but this time my hands do shake. The encounter with Mitch and Gary has upset me more than I'd like to admit.

Inside are four backpacks for emergencies. I hand Charlie his, which contains three different sets of fake passports for him and fake student IDs for different schools. There's also five hundred dollars cash, the equivalence of five hundred dollars in various other currencies, two prepaid phones, some tiny comm units, a secure laptop, two changes of clothes, some energy bars, and a bottle of water.

Mine holds the same basics, but no computer. I have a medical kit, too. I leave Mom's and Dad's where they are. Their packs have ammo and guns in them—in my mom's case, a Sig Sauer and a Beretta, and in my dad's case, a Ruger and a sniper rifle. While this is all standard gear for Agency employees of my parents' classification, these are not items I want to carry around Union Station. They're the spies. I'm just a kid.

Charlie and I zoom off to a ladies' room, where I force him in with me despite his protests.

"I'm not going into the girls' bathroom!" he insists.

"Yes, you are. We don't know if Mitch followed us."

He gets a mulish expression on his face, but I give him the stink eye. "C'mon, *Charlotte*. Inside." Charlie's disguise is not exactly to his liking.

He heaves a sigh, makes a face, and follows me in.

With a silent apology, I do the politically incorrect thing, and we take over the stall reserved for handicapped visitors. I figure that if a person in a wheelchair rolls in, we can vacate it immediately—but for right now, we need the room that it offers.

The zippers of the packs sound really loud in the metal-enclosed space. I hear the door to the hallway open and two sets of female feet clip-clop inside.

"So I told him," a woman's voice says, "that his behavior was totally unacceptable. I mean, who does that!"

"What a loser," the other woman says.

"No kidding . . ."

They continue to bash the unknown guy while they pee.

In the meantime, I put on a black T-shirt with holes in it, a black miniskirt, torn black tights, and combat boots. To complete the look, I slap very pale powder all over my face, ring my eyes with thick, funeral-black liner, and apply a vampy lipstick so dark that it looks black too. Because I suck at putting on makeup, I actually have to fix the smears I make with the eraser of my math pencil. I can imagine Aunt Sophie laughing her gorgeous blond butt off.

Once Soph tried to teach me how to use lip liner.

Only once. Let's leave it at that.

Next comes the wig in—you guessed it—Goth black. It's chin length with bangs, and I have to tuck my real hair up into a cap that feels sort of like a nylon stocking. I tug the wig into place and make sure it's on my head evenly.

I wrap two black-leather, studded cuffs around my wrists, and loop a thick silver chain around my neck, then double it before fastening. The icing on top is the nose ring, which doesn't go all the way through my skin but is pretty gross to insert. And does it ever feel weird.

Poor Charlie has put on a plaid miniskirt and a white top with a navy sweater over it. He sits on the floor and pulls on white knee socks and penny loafers. I add the blond, curly wig to his head, and he sticks his tongue out at me.

"You look like a vampire," he says.

"Yeah? Well you look like Little Bo Peep."

"Do not. Where are my sheep?"

"They'll meet up with us later." I wink at him.

Charlie rolls his eyes.

We stuff our old clothes into the backpacks and rezip them. Then we empty and ditch our school bags, take the escalator up to the street level, and get a taxi.

"Where to?" The driver looks bored as he meets my eyes in the rearview mirror.

"Providence Street. Taking the kid to her aunt's."

He uses the mirror to look from one of us to the other. I know we make a pretty odd pair—Little Miss Sunshine and the gloomy, glowering Goth chick. But he says nothing. DC is a big city—people usually mind their own business. We drive for what seems like forever, the meter running the whole way. We crawl through traffic, dodging limousines, tourist buses, and government vehicles with diplomatic plates. Finally we get to Providence Street, which is on the outskirts of town.

"What's the address?" our driver inquires.

"Just up here, that white house with the blue shutters on the right."

Taxi man pulls up to the curb, and I look at the eye-popping total on the meter. It would take me hours of babysitting to come up with that. But I dig into the backpack and pull out the amount I need, plus a 10 percent tip. I hand over the bills, and little "Charlotte" and I climb out of the cab.

"Thanks," I say.

He nods.

Charlie and I start up the front walkway of a house we've never seen before. I pause about halfway up and pretend to look in my backpack for a nonexistent key.

Once the taxi is out of sight, we hoof it to the sidewalk and walk the few blocks to the Comfort Inn & Suites, which is our real, pre-arranged rendezvous point with our parents.

The clerk is a prim young Asian woman who eyes my Goth getup with barely repressed disapproval. Given the opportunity, I am positive that she would vault over the reception desk with a wet wipe and clean all the black off my face before checking us in. She demands to see some sort of identification.

I dig out one of my fake IDs and its matching credit card and push them across the counter to her. The photo on it makes me look like a stone-cold killer, so I do my best to adopt the same expression. She looks from me to Charlie and back again, much as the cab-driver did. "You're . . . together?"

"Yup." I sneer at her, curling my lip. "Charlotte's my cousin. She's the flower girl in my dad's wedding tomorrow. I'm a freakin' bridesmaid." I produce a disgusted snort. "Me. Of all people. And the new step-monster is making me wear *pink*."

The clerk—her name tag says Serena—blinks and has the grace to look a little sorry for me. "Pink? It's not tulle, is it?"

I poke my tongue into my cheek. "Worse. Shiny polyester satin."

"Dear God." Serena clicks around on her computer keyboard and purses her lips. "You know, I think I can upgrade you. . . ."

"And the shoes? Dyed to match, with these unbelievably ugly white roses clipped to the toes."

At this Serena actually shudders. "Yes—I can give you a junior suite for the price of a single. How's that?"

"Awesome," I say, grinning. Then I realize that this sounds out of character. I disappear the grin and substitute a scowl. "That'll work."

"I'll throw in a coupon to the restaurant next door too. Buy one dinner, get one free."

"Thank you." I realize I'm starving, and Charlie probably is too. We can get big, juicy burgers to go while we're waiting for Mom and Dad. I keep trying to go vegetarian, but it doesn't work. I guess I'm a die-hard carnivore.

She gives us our key cards, and after going next door to

get the burgers, we find our way to room 308. We dump our backpacks on the sofa in the little sitting area and collapse on the two double beds. I'm so tired. That's the flip side of adrenaline—when it wears off, you're exhausted. And, of course, I've never fought off two big guys who were trying to kidnap me. Sure, I've beat my friend Kale a few times in karate matches, but that's different. It's all in the name of practice and/or fun.

Going up against Mitch and Gary? Not fun. Not even a little.

I look at my watch. It's been a full three and a half hours since Dad sent those texts to me and Charlie.

My brother yanks off his Charlotte wig but leaves on the weird hairnet/cap that holds it on his head. He looks like a small, bald scientist—until you get to the skirt.

I can tell that he's tired too. At least his anxiety seems to have faded. He slides his legs off the bed and goes to his backpack to get the computer, which he takes back to the bed with him and opens. Within two minutes he's surfing the Internet, looking for God knows what. I hope Mom and Dad put parental controls on the thing.

Charlie's lips begin to move. He's repeating words, but I'm not sure what language they're in. German?

Mom wants him to learn it for some reason, and so he's been studying it after he finishes all his other homework. I have no idea why it's important for a seven-year-old to learn German.

Mom was desperate for me to learn Russian, because she speaks it herself and she wanted us to be able to "chat." But the Cyrillic alphabet defies understanding. I stare at Charlie as he studies, wondering what planet he came from and how we're related. Sometimes I wish I could be a brother to him, instead of a sister. My brother badly needs a normal male role model.

Where are our parents? It's been four hours now. What could be holding them up? This is the third and last rendezvous point. What if they were caught by a foreign government and are being held and interrogated? Oh, my God—what if they were executed?

Calm down, Kari. Don't jump to conclusions.

But what am I supposed to think? I pinch the Bran Castle charm between my finger and thumb. The charm indicates that they may have been in Romania at some point, but I have no idea for how long—not to mention that it could be a decoy, picked up on a previous trip. For security reasons, they can't really tell me and Charlie where they go.

What if their plane went down? What if someone shot them? Or held them at gunpoint and kidnapped them?

Another piece of Mom's advice comes to me: *Quiet your mind by taking it somewhere else.*

So I lie on the bed and pretend that I'm floating on a raft in the deep blue ocean, maybe off the coast of Barbados. I've never been there, but it sounds exotic and peaceful. I concentrate on feeling the sun warm my body, and the gentle rocking of the waves. Charlie's low muttering becomes the breeze, and the cycling AC becomes the sound of the tide cresting and lapping at the shore.

I'm almost asleep when Luke shows up. He's swum all the way out to my raft from the shore, and he has no shirt on. He's tanned and muscular and so freakin' hot that I'm really afraid I might—accidentally—lick him. I push myself up onto my elbows and greet him with a huge smile. . . .

And then someone says, in a hateful British accent, "Seen a dentist lately, love?"

Aaargh! My eyes fly open. Evan has no right to show up in my daydream!

But since he has, I take the opportunity to check on my brother. No need, really—he's still studying on the bed next to mine—but it makes me feel better.

I close my eyes again to see if I can go back to the coast of Barbados, to Luke with his shirt off. There . . . okay, I have the sun on my skin again, and the blue water surrounds me, and I relax. Someone is swimming toward me, doing a beautiful crawl through the waves. It's Luke, but when he takes a breath, his face is turned away from me.

I check my swimsuit—a two-piece with a rainbow-striped bandeau top and black bottom—to make sure nothing inappropriate is hanging out. Then I look up and smile at Luke, except he's not there.

Next I hear the badly hummed theme to *Jaws* and my raft overturns with a splash, courtesy of Evan. I capsize into the ocean, and my mouth fills with salt water as he mocks me and laughs.

My eyes fly open, and I'm back on the pastel commercial bedspread that the Comfort Inn must order by the hundreds. Charlie is still muttering in German. The AC unit clangs as it cycles off.

But I swear I can taste salt in my mouth. And if I ever get to return to that daydream, I'm going to push Evan's head underwater and drown him.

Chapter Four

Two more hours have gone torturously by. It's like waiting for frozen molasses to drip through an hourglass . . .
and all the while horrible images blink through my head.
Dad, with scarlet blooming over his jacket as he's shot
while riding a motorbike on the streets of Prague. Mom,
writhing on the floor of a Sardinian café, poisoned hor-
ribly by a pill dropped into her espresso. Both of them,
blown to unrecognizable pieces by a car bomb in Tel Aviv.

The sick movie reel in my mind is bad enough, but I
can't even acknowledge my fear aloud—I have to stay
strong and upbeat for Charlie.

I have to stop obsessing or I'll go nuts. But the walls are
closing in on me. Everything is symmetrical in the room,
from the placement of the beds to the bad pictures of
ducks hung over them, from the identical reading lamps
to the nightstands.

It all contributes to this feeling I have that we've accidently fallen into a bad B movie. It's one thing to have a family plan in place in case of a Code Black scenario— it's quite another thing to be following that plan blindly, without a script of what's happening behind the scenes.

To distract myself from worrying about my parents, I obsess about Luke instead. I cannot believe that I grinned at him with mashed up M&M's in my mouth, like some kind of brain-dead jack-o'-lantern. What is wrong with me?

I try to imagine what my teeth must have looked like and cringe. Really, how gross was it? I decide that I need to do an experiment, and it gives me a great excuse to get out of this claustrophobic room, even if only for a couple of minutes.

"Charlie, do you want a candy bar out of the vending machine?"

He looks up absently from the computer screen. "Huh?"

I repeat the question and his eyes brighten. "Yeah. A Snickers."

"What's the magic word?"

"Abracadabra?" Charlie asks, the little imp.

"Dude."

"*Please*," he says, rolling his eyes behind those miniature horn-rims.

I nod. "Okay, I'll go get us some sugar. But do not open this door to anyone but me. Got it?"

I pick up my key card and exit the room, stretching my legs as I go down the hallway toward the little alcove where the hotel has the ice and vending machines. As promised, I get a Snickers for Charlie . . . and Peanut M&M's for me.

Yes, I know that I'm ridiculous. Back in the room I give Charlie his candy bar and go into the bathroom. I close the door behind me, then open the bag of M&M's. I put four into my mouth at once and chew a few times. Then I smile at myself in the mirror.

Oh. My. God. The results are disgusting.

Seen a dentist lately, love? Evan's voice echoes, once again, in my pea brain.

I cannot believe I did that in front of Luke.

Can lightning strike me now? Can the floor open up and swallow me?

I choke down the chocolate in my mouth and toss the rest of the bag in the trash.

I stare at my Goth self in the mirror. Underneath all that white powder, I am beet red.

How can I recover from this? Luke must think I'm so gross. So unattractive.

And Evan . . . I cannot stand the jerk. I mean, what kind of person wears custom-tailored shirts to *school*? A pretentious person, that's who. And that accent of his? It does *not* make him smarter than everyone else. Which I will be *happy* to tell him the next time I have the bad luck to bump into him.

I run some water into a Comfort Inn plastic cup and swish it around in my mouth. Then I take one of their pristine white washcloths and scrub like a maniac at my teeth. I rinse again. I grin like a mule into the mirror to see if there are any renegade M&M particles still stuck anywhere. Nope.

I resolve to use some of my emergency dollars (only a few) on Crest Whitestrips so that the next time I see Luke, I will blind him with my smile.

Next I lather up my face with soap and get every speck of the gruesome Goth makeup off my skin. It's a relief to look normal again, even if our circumstances are anything but.

More awful film stills spin in a kaleidoscope of horror through my mind: my dad lying in a street with his skull bashed in; my mom bound hand and foot and hanging from a hook while some assassin beats her; both of them riddled with bullets in the middle of an icy field, splashes of their bright red blood marking the snow.

My hands tremble uncontrollably as I hold a towel to my face.

Stop it, Kari!

When I leave the bathroom, Charlie has finished both his Snickers bar and his German. He's moved on to something lighter: the history of electricity and the theory of AC circuits.

I make my brother close the laptop at eight p.m. and brush his teeth with a toothbrush I got from the front desk. He gets into bed in his T-shirt and boxers, removes his horn-rims, and folds them before putting them on the bedside table. He really is like a tiny banker—I can picture him doing the same thing thirty years and a hundred pounds from now. I kiss his forehead and turn out the bedside lights before going to the sitting room side of the suite.

"Kari?" he asks. "Do you think Mom and Dad will be here by morning?"

"Yeah. I'm positive, kiddo. Remember, they could be in Uzbekistan for all we know, traveling on back country roads in a 1963 Fiat. That could take a while."

"Or maybe they're on a camel in Saudi Arabia, and they have to cross a desert."

We fall easily into one of our favorite games: Where in the World Are Mom and Dad? "Or maybe they're in Spain, running with the bulls."

"Or maybe," says Charlie, "they're in Venice, making their getaway in a gondola."

"I like that one," I tell him. I sit beside him on the bed and squeeze his hand. "And they'll bring us those little chocolate Baci from Italy when they come home."

"Baci?" Charlie's eyelids are drooping.

I remember that it's been three or four years since our parents went to Italy, so Charlie would have been pretty young. "Those chocolates with the messages inside. Kind of like Dove Promises. *Baci* means 'kisses' in Italian." Ha. That's, like, the only foreign word I know. That and *bonjour.*

My brother looks forlorn for a moment. "I want real kisses. One from Mom, and one from Dad."

"Oh, sweetie." I gather him up in a hug. "I know. But they're doing really important jobs for our country." It sounds a little corny when I say that out loud, but I mean it.

"Our parents," I continue, "are the true heroes. They're the ones who do the dirty work behind the scenes that nobody else wants to do. They take incredible risks. They combat, well, evil. Yeah, that sounds dramatic—but it's the honest truth." Sometimes I am so proud of our parents that my heart feels like it's too big for my chest.

"I guess it makes it worth it that they're gone all the time . . . kind of. But I miss them," Charlie says, drowsiness creeping into his voice.

"Yeah, I know. Same here."

And obviously I get scared for them too, but I don't tell Charlie that. What they do is dangerous. Those guns in their emergency packs? They actually need those.

I try not to think about the fact that Mom and Dad could be in some kind of shoot-out right this minute, sitting back-to-back while bullets fly around them.

It's not likely. Most spy work is pretty low key, believe it or not. There's a lot of surveillance and computer tracking and peering at activity beamed to the U.S. by satellite. Depending on what cover they're using—say, foreign diplomat—they might just be writing reports and schmoozing at cocktail parties while they slowly gather information. I know this because they've told me, probably just to allay my fears.

Charlie emits the tiniest, cutest snore, and I know he's out for the count.

I wonder what my friend Kale is up to. I want to text him, but it may not be safe—given the situation my friends' phones could be monitored, and it's best not to put my new number on anyone's radar screen unless it's truly necessary.

I sprawl full-length on the couch, stare at the textured white ceiling, and try to count the bumps. If I stay in this room much longer, I'll go nuts. At last, after counting 259 tiny plaster bumps, my exhaustion kicks in and I fall asleep in all my clothes.

As if my brain knows that I can't take any more worry, it floods my dreams with images of Luke. Luke runs—and wins—a track meet in nothing but his tan and a tiny pair of blue shorts . . . while I cheer and scream from the stands. He waves and blows me a kiss from the finish line, and I give him a huge gold cup that we drink champagne out of later. I guess in my dreams I'm not underage.

I must also be extremely rich, because before I know it, Luke and I are driving through Monaco in a Ferrari— we're racing in the Grand Prix. I am wearing cat's-eye sunglasses and a white silk scarf tied around my neck. We are impossibly glamorous.

He's soon kissing me on the deck of a yacht in the Mediterranean, while the warm breeze caresses us. We're lying on the bow, rocking rhythmically as we cut through the water. He rolls me on top of him, and I'm touching every hard inch of him, my body molding to his.

"I want you, Kari," he whispers into my hair. "Right now."

I press into him shamelessly . . . only instead of pressing back, he flattens and fades away. I wake, mortified to realize that I'm making out with the sagging, nubby couch—pressing my lips into the dent that hundreds of butts have made. Nice.

But I'm so tired, worn out with stress, that sleep reclaims me before I do more than turn my head.

In the morning I wake with the mother of all cricks in my neck and a sore back, not to mention furry teeth. My watch says it's 7:33 a.m. Charlie is still sleeping peacefully, and there's no sign of our parents.

I slide off the couch, use the bathroom, and admire the woven tweedy texture embedded in my cheek. Couch pillows? They're not so soft. Then I stagger over to the double bed that's mine and crawl under the covers for another few hours.

When I wake up the second time, Charlie's tapping away at the keyboard of the laptop, glasses slipping down his nose. His hair is flattened on one side.

"Morning," I mumble.

"Almost afternoon."

Sure enough, the clock now says 11:43. It's been a full twenty-four hours since we got the texts from Dad. Fear forms a dull ache in my head.

I shower quickly, Goth myself up again, and tell Charlie that I'm going to go find us some food. He's totally absorbed in—I glance quickly at the screen—how a camera works and how photography has evolved over the past one hundred years or so.

I stuff some money and one of the prepaid phones into my jacket pocket and head for the door. "Don't open this for anyone but me," I remind my brother again.

He rolls his eyes.

"And it'd be good if you cleaned up and got dressed, kiddo, just in case we have to leave quickly."

He nods, and then I lose him once again to the laptop and the infinite jungle of theories and ideas out there—where he's like a curious monkey, swinging from vine to vine and concept to concept.

I take the elevator down, breeze past Serena at the desk, and head out to the street. Even though I know my Goth disguise has eradicated any sign of Kari Andrews, prep-school girl, I am nervous to the point of paranoia. Mitch and Gary may be anywhere, and they may also not be the only Agency people trying to track down me and Charlie.

Twenty feet to the left of the hotel doors, there's a man roughly Mitch's height and weight pawing through a garbage receptacle for cans. I freeze for a moment, trying to decide whether or not he's a plant.

Across the street is an old lady dragging one of those grocery carts on wheels, two paper sacks full of goods inside. Does she have a Beretta in there along with her baguette?

And a dark-suited businessman strides toward me from the right, a Burberry raincoat draped over one arm and a briefcase in the other. For all I know he's got a stun gun in his pocket and a government-issued SUV around the corner.

I stand right outside the doors of the Comfort Inn and pretend to text on my phone until he's well down the street. The lady with the shopping cart disappears around a corner. And the guy at the garbage can moves down a block to the next set of trash bins.

I let out a long, slow breath that I hadn't been aware I was holding. Then I head west and walk a couple of blocks, keeping my head down and scanning every car I pass for signs that it's unlocked and easy to, um, borrow.

It's not stealing if you return the vehicle when you're done with it, Mom's voice says in my head.

My dad taught me at an early age how to tie my shoes, how to ride a bike, and how to "borrow" a car. So I look for a low-end, older model that won't attract attention.

There's an old movie theater a couple of blocks away, and I know the first matinee show of the day starts soon. I walk to the pay lot near it and observe as an older, probably retired couple gets out of an unremarkable 2001 Hyundai Sonata. They lock it and walk toward the theater. I trail behind them and fiddle with my phone as they ask for tickets to a foreign film that ends two hours and twenty-odd minutes from now. Perfect.

Once the theater swallows them up, I make my way back to their car. I stand next to it and scan the street both ways, still half expecting to see Mitch pop up, while looking for a set of imaginary keys in my messenger bag. What I pull out instead is a set of lock picks.

Thanks, Mom and Dad. They were a great thirteenth birthday gift.

Nobody pays any attention to me. It takes me only a few nervous seconds to jimmy the door and slip into the driver's seat. Within a couple of minutes, I've cracked the steering column and hot-wired the vehicle.

The Sonata smells like dirty vinyl, wet dog, and stale cigarettes. I ease into traffic and go around the block a couple of times, checking in the rearview mirror at every turn to make sure I'm not being followed. There's no sign of a tail by Mitch, Gary, or anyone else, so I head back to the other side of town and pull into the parking lot of a Laundromat that's close to Kennedy Prep. I walk inside, pretend to check on a dryer full of clothes, and then make my way to the east wall, where there's a long bulletin board plastered with community notices: fliers for a lost dog, an ad that a 2003 Buick Regal is for sale, phone numbers for a pet-sitting service, et cetera.

I search through all the business cards and scraps of paper on the board until I see what I'm looking for:

Guitar Lessons from Larry. Basic guitar for students
K–12 taught by a qualified graduate student
at GWU's Carson School of Music.

Oh, that's very cute, Rita! Luke's last name is Carson. I shake my head but can't help a grin. My steps are lighter as I go back to my borrowed Hyundai and drive it to a nearby Kinko's. There I buy a session on one of their computers and create a flier in response to hers.

Need a Chemistry Tutor?
Union grad
Rate: $10–12.00/hour
Call 215-Chem, ext. 50

Rita will understand exactly what I mean: to meet tomorrow, October 10, at twelve noon, at the Starbucks (shop 215) at Union Station, which is at 50 Massachusetts Avenue.

Rita desperately wants to be a spy—like my parents. A long time ago—eight years, to be exact—Rita, who's the daughter of Senator Jordan, was kidnapped in a scheme to extort money from her dad. To make a long story short, my parents were the ones who rescued her from the creeps who took her, and they brought her to our house while they helped to round up the rest of the kidnapping ring.

Poor Rita was traumatized and couldn't sleep alone, so she shared my room while she stayed with us—and we've been best friends ever since. When I tell you that she *worships* my parents, I am not kidding . . . and the bottom line is that hers kind of ignore her. I mean, they love their daughter, but they're always at some charity event or on the campaign trail, or her mom is having "work" done again—not that she needs it. She's this gorgeous Indian woman, and she sort of floats everywhere she goes.

Rita doesn't get her fashion sense from her mom, though—it's very edgy and all her own. It's a little funky, a little neon, a lot of black, and hard to describe. She'll pair a really high-end item—jewelry or a hat or a couture bustier—with trashy, holey jeans. Or a ripped T-shirt over a purple bra with six-hundred-dollar Donna Karan black pants that her mom didn't want anymore. I can't tell you how she does it or why it works, but she always looks like she stepped off a runway.

Rita has about ten pairs of prescription, designer glasses that are the signature, pièce de résistance of her look. The black-and-white Diors, for example. Or the pink Chanels. The deep ruby-red Marc Jacobs pair . . . they all make her look really smart—which she is—but also sophisticated, like a buyer for a hip, Chelsea boutique. If you met Rita, you'd never guess that she's one of the best computer hackers out there, because she doesn't fit the nerd profile.

I drive back to the Laundromat and put up my flier. Then I return my borrowed car after picking up sandwiches, and head back to the hotel, praying that nobody has tracked us down and that Charlie is still where I left him.

To my relief, he is.

Chapter Five

At noon I stride into the Starbucks like I own it, and my attitude says: What are the rest of these losers doing here? I pay cash for a latte and slouch toward Rita, into the darkest corner of the place. I'm in my Goth getup, and I'm starting to feel at home in it, sneering at everyone. It's a good way to relieve my anxiety.

Rita is wearing the pink Chanel glasses, which set off her dark skin to perfection, with a motorcycle jacket and skinny jeans. In her ears she's put a diamond stud (left lobe) and a pair of dangly silver handcuffs (right lobe). She's got on killer black stiletto boots that make my feet hurt just looking at them, and I think they're Jimmy Choo, meaning that it would take me two years to save up for them. Rita and her mom have a totally different idea of what's normal to spend on clothes than I do.

I'm pleased that Rita doesn't recognize me until I sit

down opposite her and smirk. She does a double take, a slow rescan of my appearance, and then nods with approval.

"Girl," she says in low tones, "*everyone* is looking for you and Charlie. You've been declared missing children."

I'm glad we dressed Charlie as a girl. "Have you heard anything about my parents?"

Rita stares at me blankly, and I realize that she doesn't know they're MIA—or what started all this. "Rita, they got in touch with us yesterday, a Code Black message. That's why I left art class and disappeared. We've tried to meet them in three different places, but they haven't shown up. I don't know where they are or what's going on."

She scans the tables around us before answering. "Look, all I know is that Senator Dad got a phone call last night. I don't know who it was, but I heard him repeat the words 'suspicious activity?' and then 'the Andrewses'?' I couldn't hear much, but he said, 'No, certainly not. Why do you ask?' Then he stayed on the phone for a few minutes, just saying 'Uh-huh. Okay . . . I see' and stuff like that. When he got off the phone, he seemed very weirded out. Distracted."

"Did you ask him who called?"

Rita nods. "I tried. He said, 'Nobody.' Then he asked me if I'd seen you or Charlie. I hadn't, and that's what I told him. When I asked if something was going on with your family, he told me no, no and not to worry about it. But he looked stressed, and I think he was lying to me."

I take a sip of the latte, even though I don't want it. It's more a prop than anything else. "Do you think he knows where my parents are? Or if something has happened to them?"

She shakes her head. Her high, spiky ponytail waves back and forth. "He seemed shocked at the call. Clueless. Then stressed, like I said."

I think for a moment. "Rita, does your dad tape his calls?"

She shrugs. "At the office, probably. At home, no."

"I *have* to find out what's going on."

Rita raises her right eyebrow. "So, what, you're going to waterboard my dad?"

I give a weak chuckle.

"Bug my house?"

I purse my lips.

"Don't even think about it," Rita says, shaking her finger at me.

"But—"

"No. I'm not saying I couldn't figure out how to do it, but I am not bugging my own parents' phones or house. Sorry."

I'm not sure I mentioned that she's scary-good when it comes to most technology—and in her zeal to become a spy, like my parents, she's . . . explored . . . a lot of it. That's probably a polite verb to use.

"Rita, somehow I need access to Agency data." I toss this at her like a liver snap to a starving Pomeranian.

"You're asking me to hack into the Pentagon?" There's a sparkle in her eyes, despite her dubious tone.

"Well . . . not exactly. I'm not sure it's possible."

"Is there a Pentagon or Agency mainframe? One that

holds every single piece of important U.S. data? It's highly unlikely. And even if something like that existed, we wouldn't have a clue where to look once we're on it. But if we had access to an individual who was highly placed and had top secret clearance . . . and let's say that individual had a laptop . . . and I got to have a hot date with that laptop, well, then possibilities arise."

"Possibilities, huh." The only one I can think of who has a truly primo position? Well, it's Luke and Lacey Carson's dad, the director of the Agency.

"Are you thinking of the same person I'm thinking of?" Rita asks.

I nod. "We have to talk to Luke."

"Do you think he'll help us?"

"I sure hope so," I say grimly. "Because I don't know where else to turn." Aunt Sophie maybe? She could at least give us a clue and a place to stay. I'm afraid to go home in case Mitch is waiting there.

Rita's talking, but I don't take in the words, because out of the corner of my eye, I see Evan sitting at a table on the opposite wall of Starbucks. And he's staring at us. I turn and narrow my eyes at him . . . and the smart-ass *winks* at me.

Panic rises in my throat, and I have to force it back down. There is absolutely no way that Evan has recognized me in this Goth persona. From my combat boots to my black chin-length hair, from my torn fishnets to my bite-your-head-off dark lipstick, I am nothing like the conservative, uniformed Kari Andrews he knows on a day-to-day basis.

I sneer at Evan, looking him up and down as if to say, *I eat prep-school wankers like you for breakfast. With Tabasco.*

He leans back in his chair, lacing his fingers behind his head, and grins. His expression says clearly, *You know you want me.* Arrogant jerk. My only comfort is that if he does by some crazy coincidence recognize me, he is so self-absorbed that he probably watches his own biceps in the mirror instead of the news. And he cuts class so much that he won't have heard any gossip about Charlie and me missing.

And honestly? The guy would wink at anything in a skirt. Anything with two legs and any sort of bumps in the torso area. Let's face it: Evan Kincaid would wink at a rubber blow-up doll. He'd take one on a date and never realize that his companion didn't say a word, because he'd be talking about him*self* too much.

"You haven't listened to a single word out of my mouth," Rita says, clearly offended.

"Sorry. Do not look right now, but Evan Narcissus Kincaid is right across the room. I don't think he recognizes me, but I'm sure he does you. We need to get out of here."

Rita nods, the picture of cool. "Kari, he's not that bad."

I slug down some more of my now-cold latte. "Yes, he is."

She shrugs. "But he's nice to look at."

"Whatever."

Rita digs into her Prada handbag for a box of mints and offers me one. "Okay, when do you want to meet next?"

"Today, at Kennedy," I say, taking a mint. "Around four p.m. by the back parking lot. Luke should be finishing up track practice then."

"Okay." She peers around furtively. "You leave first. I'll say hello to Evan and then wait five minutes."

"Rita, I doubt that's necessary."

"We have to follow good tradecraft," she insists.

I roll my eyes. "Yeah . . . you're right. So I left a coded message in Evan's silk Skivvies. You should go feel around for it."

Rita balls up a napkin and throws it at me.

I smirk at her and leave Starbucks for Subway, where I get Charlie a six-inch meatball sandwich on wheat with extra provolone, just the way he likes it.

On the way back to the hotel I stop at a miraculously working pay phone and use it gingerly after scrubbing the receiver with a wet wipe. I'm not obsessive-compulsive about germs or anything, but pay phones are disgusting.

I dial Aunt Sophie's number. Sophie's not really our aunt, but she's a close family friend, and my mom's like her older sister. They met when Soph started college at Georgetown—Mom was her alumna mentor.

Sophie is awesome. She's an international freelance photographer, and she's beautiful. She reminds me of a Bond girl. She looks like a sexpot, even in cargo pants and an old T-shirt. It's her long, silver-blond hair, her curves, and the way she moves. Sometimes I think Sophie could kill a man between her thighs, like Sergeant Onnatop in *GoldenEye*.

Sophie doesn't pick up. She's probably out of town on assignment. I leave her a message. "Soph, it's Kari. Call me when you get this. I need your help." I give her the number of my prepaid phone and pray that she's heading back soon from wherever she is. Sophie is the only adult we can trust, at this point. And she's got all kinds of contacts.

When I arrive back at the Comfort Inn, Charlie is still absorbed in odd subjects on the laptop. He is showered and dressed once again as Charlotte, but he's ditched the wig, which is hot and scratchy. I can't say I blame him. I whip off my own once the door is closed behind me, and I make sure the DO NOT DISTURB sign is up.

I can't believe Charlie isn't going stir-crazy or nuts with anxiety, but he's such a well-adjusted kid. He's happy to have his meatball sub and devours it in between asking me obscure questions.

"Do you know what a joule is?"

"Like an emerald or a sapphire or a diamond?"

"No, silly. J-o-u-l-e. It's a unit of energy."

"Oh. I think I like the other kind better." I smile at him.

"It's very cool," he says seriously.

I nod. "Cool joules."

He explains to me the scientific concepts he's taken in today, and I try to listen, but my thoughts are elsewhere.

What did the unknown caller say to Senator Jordan regarding my parents and "suspicious activities"? Are they being accused or framed for something? Where are they?

When will Sophie get back and call me?

How will Luke take it when Rita and I pop out of nowhere and ask him for help? Will he report me to the police, or will he be cool about things? He is kind of a Boy Scout—which I love about him—but that means I'm taking a big risk.

"Can we go get some ice cream?" Charlie asks.

"Sure. But let's wait for a little while. I don't want you to eat too much and get sick, kiddo."

"You sound just like Mom," he says.

I probably do.

The clock clearly hates me, because it is taking forever for the hands to turn around and around and tell me that it's time to leave, to borrow another car. By the time the stupid thing says it's three fifteen, I'm ready to jump out of my skin.

I leave Charlie reading about alchemy and tell him I'll be back soon. I head a couple of blocks away and circle around to find an appropriate car to take. I've decided on a gray Ford Escort that's neatly tucked between two large SUVs when I spot a harried-looking woman waiting at a bus stop on the opposite corner. She doesn't stand out in any way, except that the wind blows her hair back from her face, revealing an earpiece and a small cord that travels from it down the inside of her collar.

Still, I'm not convinced that she's surveilling me in particular until I "accidentally" drop my backpack and curse loudly. Though I know she's heard me, she doesn't look in my direction.

All the tiny hairs on the nape of my neck stand up, and I know I've been made. I know it even before I turn sixty degrees and spot Mitch, wearing a dark baseball cap and aviator sunglasses. He starts to run toward me.

I whirl in the opposite direction, only to find Gary Gray Suit headed my way as well. All three of them are closing in on me in a triangle.

In a split-second decision, I sprint right at the woman. She's not much bigger than I am, and I gamble that she's the weak spot here, since she's not familiar with my skill set.

Her eyes widen slightly and her hand slips inside her jacket. I can't let her get to a gun, if that's what it is. I launch my body into the air, right foot forward. I slam my clunky combat boot into her wrist. She cries out, spins sideways, loses her balance.

I grab the wide leather strap of her purse, yank it hard, and pull her down onto the sidewalk. I don't even break stride as I vault over her and run like hell.

Fast footsteps come from behind.

Mitch can, and will, outrun me.

My options: none.

Only the thought of Charlie makes me do what I do next.

Directly ahead is a guy on a Harley, stopped at a red light.

As the light goes green, I fly toward him—literally fly—and land straddled over the back of his bike. The guy almost falls over, but braces fast with his foot.

"I have a gun!" I scream in his ear. "Get me out of here! Go!"

He takes half a second to blink in disbelief.

I jab my small flashlight into his kidney, hard.

He shoots forward, just as Mitch grabs my shoulder.

The fabric of my top rips, but I ignore that and clutch the stranger around the middle as he accelerates.

"Go north!" I yell.

He nods.

I can see only the lower half of his face in the rearview mirror, his lips thin and his jaw tense. "I won't hurt you," I shout into his ear. "There's a man after me—I have to lose him."

He nods again. He definitely saw Mitch try to pull me off the back of his bike. His mouth relaxes, infinitesimally, as he decides he's a savior and not a victim.

I wish I could have him take me all the way to Kennedy Prep, but chances are that the Agency is already running his plates, thanks to Mitch, and will be questioning him within a couple of hours.

So I have him drop me in a residential area where it'll be easy for me to borrow another car.

"Thanks," I say, as I slip off the bike. "I wish I could explain."

He just looks at me and shakes his head. "One question."

"Yeah?"

"Are you okay?"

I nod. "Like I said, I just needed to get away from that guy."

"Should I call the cops?"

"No!"

He shakes his head again. "All right. I won't ask." He pauses, looking at me. Then he fishes a small, black leather wallet out of his back pocket and hands me a plain white card with a number on it. "If you need anything in the future, if you're in trouble like this again, you can call this number."

It's my turn to blink. "Okay . . ."

He revs the bike, and then he's gone—before I can even ask his name.

Chapter Six

I walk a couple of blocks to calm my nerves and make sure I'm not being followed. I wonder about the strange guy with nerves of steel and no name, but worry for my parents soon pushes him out of my mind. I'm just glad he was at the right place at the right time.

As soon as I've caught my breath, I call Charlie to check on him—I'm petrified that Mitch and company know which hotel I came out of.

"Hey, sis," he says, sounding distracted.

"Hey, kiddo. Whatcha doing?"

"Reading about the jet stream," he says.

Of course he is. "Listen, put on all your Charlotte stuff, even the wig. Stay in it, okay?"

"Why?"

"And keep that 'Do Not Disturb' sign on the door."

"Yup. Why?"

"Because I just saw Mitch," I tell him, editing heavily. "There are a bunch of hotels in this area, so I don't think he knows which one I came out of, but still—be careful. I'll be back this afternoon to get you, and we'll move."

"Okay."

"Don't even go to the vending machine. You'll have to drink tap water. Promise?"

"Yes."

"I love you. Be back soon."

I hang up, relieved, and check out a few vehicle possibilities before borrowing an old green Honda Civic. It looks like something that belongs to someone's assistant, a person who (I hope) won't need it back until around five. The driver has left a wool fedora-style hat in the passenger seat, so I put it on to hide my Goth hair.

I merge into traffic, horrendous as usual, and crawl in the direction of Kennedy Prep. As long as we don't come to a dead stop, I should be okay on time, in spite of my little adventure. At the most I'll be five minutes late, and track practice runs over a lot.

When I finally pull into the parking lot, I have to snort, because Rita is draped over the hood of her car, eyes closed, looking like an intellectual biker model ready for a photo shoot.

I pull the Civic into a vacant parking spot, cut the engine, ditch the hat, and get out. I glance over to where the track team is running drills on the field, and enjoy drooling over Luke's legs from afar. I also note the way the damp fabric of his shorts clings to his buns. What can I say? Rita opens her eyes, slides off her car, and rolls her eyes.

"Don't trip over your tongue," she says. "It's like a red carpet, leading all the way to your heart."

"You're funny." *Not.*

"Where'd you get the stellar wheels?"

"Borrowed 'em."

Rita smirks.

Coach blows his whistle and indicates that the team should stretch out. I'm only human—I enjoy that, too. But I'm tense. I'm starting to wonder just how you ask a guy you don't know all that well for access to his dad's laptop so that you can hack it for what might be state secrets.

Seriously. Just what am I supposed to say here?

Coach gives the team a few minutes and then blows his whistle again. They're free to go . . . all except Luke. Coach waves Luke over to talk to him about something, and Rita and I duck behind her car until all the other guys are gone.

Part of me is glad for the delay, because it gives me time to come up with a couple of nice, casual lines.

Me: *Hey, Luke. How's it going?*

Him: *Who are you?*

Oh yeah. I'm still all Gothed up. He won't even recognize me. But he'll recognize Rita. And Rita will convince him that I'm me, underneath all this gloom and doom.

So let's try this again.

Me: *Hi, Luke. It's Kari, under here.*

Him: *Kari? Oh, hey . . . we have to call the police and report that you're found.*

Me: *No, no, no—don't do that!*

Him: *Why not?*

I gulp. "Rita, what should I do? I have no clue what to say to him."

"I don't know, Kari. But you better make up your mind, because here he comes."

Luke is headed toward us, all hot, sweaty, and fine almost-six-feet of him.

And I am still without a clue. But at least I don't have Peanut M&M's on my teeth.

Luke smells like clean sweat and fresh-cut grass. He still has droplets of perspiration dotting his forehead and temples when he reaches us, and his hair is damp and spiky from practice. All I can think of is that this must be how he looks when he comes out of the shower, with only a towel wrapped around his waist.

I'm probably panting at him like a puppy, because he gives me a casual glance and then looks away as if he's a little embarrassed.

"Hi, Rita," he says. "Who's your friend?"

"It's Kari," she tells him in a theatrical whisper.

Luke does a double take. "Kari? As in Andrews?"

I nod.

"Oh my God—you're okay!" he exclaims. "You look—so different."

"Yeah." I gesture ruefully at my clothes.

"I've been really worried about you, and I'll bet your parents are too. Do you know it's been all over the news that you and Charlie are missing? I even looked for you myself, in every hangout I could think of around school."

Luke's been worried about me. Wow. And he tried to find me? A warm glow envelops my heart.

Immediately he says, "We should let the cops know that you're safe—"

"Negative." Rita shakes her head.

Luke's eyebrows draw together. "What do you mean? Haven't you seen a television lately?"

"Please," I say. "*Please* do *not* tell anyone that you have seen me. Promise."

"But—"

"Luke, it's really important," Rita tells him. "Nobody can know."

"My parents are missing," I blurt. "And I think they're in trouble. I have to find them—I have to help them—and if the police take me and Charlie into custody as minors, then I can't do that."

Luke stares from me to Rita and back. He takes a deep breath. "Why don't you start from the beginning?"

I summarize what's going on as best I can, while he listens.

"Your parents work for the Agency?" he asks.

"Yes. And they're not in human resources or accounting, if you know what I mean."

He nods. "Wow. I had no idea. My dad never told me. But then, he wouldn't." He laces his fingers behind his neck and stretches out his shoulders, still trying to absorb this information.

I nod. "And so—I really hate to ask you this—but I need your help."

"Of course," Luke says. He's such a good guy. "What can I do?"

I swallow hard. "Rita and I need access to your dad's work laptop."

Luke's expression changes from good-natured and

helpful to stunned and wary. "You have got to be kidding me."

"I wish." I stand my ground, even though I'd love to tell him that it's all a big joke.

"Kari—" He drags a hand down his face and laughs without humor. "You know I can't do that."

"Why not?" Rita demands.

"My dad's the freakin' director! I can't just hand over his laptop to two girls who happen to attend the same school as me."

"We know exactly who your dad is. That's why we need your help," Rita explains to him, as if he's a two-year-old—and not a very bright one.

"This isn't like hacking someone's Facebook page, Rita. We're talking about national security here." He uses the same tone with her.

"Exactly," I chime in. "My parents have worked for the Agency for twenty years. They're loyal employees, and they need help now that they're in trouble."

Luke nods. "Great. So let's go talk to my dad, and he will work through official channels to help them."

It sounds logical and reasonable—I have to admit that. But too many things aren't adding up. "No. Mitch has been with the Agency for almost as long as my parents have, and he's the one who tried to kidnap me and Charlie. The last thing I want is for Mitch or his buddy Gary Whatever to know where I am or what my movements are."

"So we tell my dad to keep things quiet," Luke says.

"I think it's a bad idea," Rita declares. "What if he only

tells one person, and that employee is the very one who's not trustworthy?"

"Luke, my parents' lives could be at stake." I hate the pleading note that enters my voice, but I can't seem to suppress it.

He closes his eyes. "You're asking me to break into a government database."

"No," Rita corrects him. "We're asking you for thirty minutes alone with your dad's laptop. You won't have anything to do with the security breach."

"Except engineering the opportunity," Luke says.

I can see guilt eating him up at the very idea. He opens his eyes but sets his jaw and flattens his lips. I'm afraid he's about to say no. I wince.

But before he can say anything, a completely unwelcome, hateful, British voice joins the conversation. "Oh, come, Lucas. You won't find a prettier reason anywhere to throw your pops under a bus."

Rita shrieks.

I almost come out of my skin.

And even Luke takes a step backward as Evan appears out of thin air. "Where the hell did you come from, dude?"

"Ah." Evan smirks and holds up an index finger. "First rule of a sneak attack: Be sneaky." He looks at each of our faces briefly, and then his gaze returns to mine. "You look as if you bit into a thundercloud, love. Indigestion?"

"Evan, what are you doing here?" I snap.

"Just happened to be in the neighborhood."

"Right. And you just happened to be at the Starbucks in Union Station too."

He looks at me with an expression of kindly tolerance. "Second rule of a sneak attack, Kari my love: Perform surveillance upon other sneaky persons before sneaking up on them."

"How did you recognize me?" I am annoyed beyond reason.

He grins a predatory male grin. "Would you really like to know?"

I am so tempted to head-butt his nose, just as I did to Mitch. But I just raise my eyebrows and wait for him to illuminate me.

"You've done a rather good job of transforming yourself, I must say. But you haven't bothered to change your gait—and it gives you away as an athlete, not a rebellious, chain-smoking night crawler who's never seen the inside of a gym."

I'm disgusted with myself, which makes me even angrier with Evan.

"That was what led me to look at you more carefully. But there's something else that you simply can't hide."

I stare stonily at him and refuse to take the bait. But Rita's dying of curiosity.

"What?" she prompts him.

His gaze slides to her for a moment and then returns to me as his smirk widens. "It's the curve of your arse, love. I'd know it anywhere."

Rita's jaw drops open.

Luke has a sudden coughing fit and smothers it in the crook of his elbow.

And I stand there mortified, unable to think of a

suitably scathing response. Finally I say, "Evan, we were actually having a private conversation. So if you don't mind . . ."

"Sod off?" he finishes helpfully.

"Yeah."

"I'm sorry to disappoint you, but I find that I have an overwhelming desire to play superspy along with the rest of you." He shoves his hands into his pockets and rocks back on his heels.

I close my eyes. That means he's heard *everything*. And I still don't know where he was hiding.

"I don't know what you're talking about," I hedge.

"Oh, I'll wager that you do. Your parents are missing, you want Lucas here to keep your secret—and better yet, to allow our lovely Larita to hack into his noble sire's laptop. Does that sum things up?"

Luke looks up at the sky and exhales. Then he looks down at his running shoes and shakes his head.

"Evan, don't you have someone else to annoy?"

"Let me think." He strokes his chin for a moment. "No. Sorry."

"We don't want you here," I say.

Luke rubs the back of his neck and carefully avoids Evan's gaze.

"I'd truly hate to have to report to the authorities that I saw you, love. But naturally, it would be only for your safety."

"You . . . you . . ." I open and close my mouth like a fish.

"Jackass?" Evan supplies helpfully. "Arsehole?"

"That doesn't even begin to cover it," I assure him. "There are no words bad enough for you."

"I find myself curiously flattered," Evan muses.

"We're wasting time," Rita breaks in. "Kari, get over it. Evan's joined the party."

She takes me aside and whispers in my ear, "And even if you don't like him, he's good eye candy."

I'm not so sure he didn't overhear this little gem.

I stare at him in disbelief as he nods and lifts a corner of his mouth at me. Then he blows on his fingernails and polishes them on his tailored shirt. "Now, where were we?"

Aaaarrrgghhh!

"We were convincing Luke that we need access to his dad's laptop," Rita says. "Because it may be the only insight we can get into what has happened to Kari's parents."

"Who are spies. Do I have that right?" Evan turns to me, his face the picture of avid interest.

I take a deep breath so that I won't hit him. Then I nod.

"Fascinating," he murmurs. "I've never met a bona fide spy. However did they get into such a profession?"

I take another deep breath and clench my fists. I glare at Rita, who looks skyward.

"Does one go to spy school?" he wonders aloud. "Does one write a thesis on surveillance?"

"Evan," I say through gritted teeth, "I don't have time to explain it to you right now. In case you didn't pick up on it, we have an urgent situation on our hands."

"Right," Evan agrees. "Well, you'll have to let me buy you a pint sometime and you can tell me all about it."

I barely restrain a growl.

Evan turns to Luke. "Terribly sorry, mate. Back to pressure-cooking you over pop's laptop."

"Like there's going to be a file on the desktop labeled 'Andrews, What Happened to Them,'" Luke says, exasperated. "Rita, you have no idea where to look, even if I did manage to give you a half hour alone with the thing."

"I happen to be very good at what I do," she says hotly, pushing the pink Chanel glasses up to the bridge of her nose.

"Of course you are," Evan soothes her. "No one's in any doubt."

Luke folds his arms across his chest. In terms of body language, it's not a good sign for our cause.

"So," Evan says. "We have a pair of vanished spies. We have, in Mitch and his counterpart, a pair of rogue agents—possibly moles, since they knew exactly where to find Kari and Charlie. Moles who are willing to go as far as kidnapping, and perhaps worse. And we have a police APB out on Kari and her brother, a well-publicized one, which suggests deliberate leaks by someone in power. I can't say that's good news."

"What if it is, though?" Luke asks. "What if it's Kari's parents who leaked the info to the cops? And they want to make sure that their kids are picked up and safe?"

I shake my head. "They already knew where to find us. We set prearranged meeting points and times, and my parents didn't make any of them. There's something really wrong." I am not pleased that pressure is forming behind my eyes, and that they're beginning to sting. I'm not a blubberer.

Luke shifts his weight from one foot to the other.

"Not to mention that the Andrewses' lives could be at stake," Rita says.

Luke looks reluctantly at me.

I'm horrified to realize that my eyes are filling, and even though I blink furiously and order the tears back to wherever they came from, a couple of them escape and roll down my Gothed-up face.

Luke takes a step toward me, his hand reaching out.

"Got something in my eye," I mutter gruffly, and use the hem of my black T-shirt to try to repair any damage to my funeral-black liner and mascara.

Evan raises an eyebrow at Luke. "You going to just stand here and let the poor girl cry, when you have the power to solve her problem?"

Luke stares at him, flinty eyed, for a long moment. Then he looks over at me and sighs.

"C'mon. Let's go."

Chapter Seven

We return my borrowed car and then pile into Luke's Grand Cherokee. Luke lives in Great Falls, in a beautiful old two-story Greek revival home. I can just picture his sister Lacey in another century. She sweeps down the curved staircase in a ball gown and takes the arm of a beau who escorts her through the white columns framing the porch and up into a waiting carriage.

Evan murmurs under his breath, "How terribly *Gone with the Wind*."

Unfortunately it's the twenty-first century, and Lacey shows no signs of leaving, since her silver BMW 335i is parked in the drive. Luke parks his Jeep next to it.

Mr. Carson's government-issue Lincoln Continental isn't anywhere to be seen, and neither is the old silver Mercedes that Luke's mom usually drives when she drops off the kids at school.

We troop into the house behind Luke, and I hope that his sister stays in her room instead of coming out to look at me like I'm some weird and disgusting species of insect. She cannot stand Rita—it's probably a fashion rivalry or something—and since I'm Rita's best friend, she despises me, too.

The house is full of antiques, and the huge kitchen has dark cherry cabinetry and a big granite-topped island in the middle. There's an apron tossed on it that says CHEF DAD across the chest and a notepad next to it. Someone has scrawled:

Gone to get filet mignon and portobello mushrooms. Will stop at package store for wine, too.

The handwriting is bold and masculine. Is it possible that we've just gotten very, very lucky?

"My dad likes to cook," Luke confirms. "My mom, not so much. She decorates."

At the back of the house, to the rear of the kitchen, is an old-fashioned study behind a set of French doors. It's lined with cherry bookshelves. A desk the size of an apartment complex presides over a big Oriental rug, and a burgundy-leather rolling chair sits behind it.

Luke enters a four-digit code into a simple keypad on the left door and opens it to let us in.

We barely spare a glance for the decor or the silver-framed photos of Mr. Carson with different presidents, senators, and other heads of state. Instead we're fixated on the laptop that sits on a leather blotter in the middle of the desk.

Rita pumps her fist into the air. "Yes!"

"Lucky break." Luke swallows nervously.

Am I the only one who thinks this is a little too good to be true? "You guys, this is awfully convenient. Almost like someone's been listening to our conversations." I shoot a narrowed glance at Evan as I say this.

His expression is as innocent as the Gerber baby's. Ha.

"Oh, Kari. Don't be paranoid," Rita retorts.

Me? She's the one who's obsessed with all the cloak-and-dagger! "I'm just saying. . . ."

But she's already behind Mr. Carson's desk, her fingers clearly itching to violate his privacy and probably several different laws. I love Rita, but she is a snoop.

Clearly Luke isn't at all comfortable with this.

"Um," he says to Rita as she opens the laptop. "Shouldn't you wear gloves or something?"

She peers at him over the pink Chanel glasses. "What, does he dust for prints every night? Is he expecting someone to hack into his computer?"

Luke flushes and turns away. "I'm going to take a shower," he says, and disappears.

I try not to think about Luke naked upstairs as Rita fishes a thumb drive out of her purse, plugs it into Director Carson's laptop, and hits the start button.

"Whoa," Evan says, looking uncomfortable all of a sudden.

"What's that?" I ask her.

She rolls her eyes at Evan, shoots me a glance from under her lashes, and chooses USB Drive as the boot-up device from the screen. "It's a different operating system."

"Holy crap," is all I can think of to say. "Why?"

"Are you really doing this?" Evan asks. "I thought you were joking."

She doesn't even spare him a glance.

"It's called Backtrack," she explains. "And it should be able to obtain Mr. Carson's password." She types some commands into the computer while I watch, very uncomfortable with this, but still desperate enough to do it.

My skin feels hot and itchy, my pulse has kicked up, and my palms are sweating.

Evan just stands like a statue, one eyebrow raised.

Rita attempts to access the hard drive directly, but it asks her for a password, which is only to be expected. She blows out a breath. "Okay, time for a little brute-forcing," she says.

"What?" I'm alarmed. "Don't hurt the machine!"

She chuckles. "I'm talking about *password* brute-forcing," she says, "not smashing the computer with a sledgehammer."

"It doesn't sound good." I fold my arms.

"Don't worry. It's fine."

Rita's fingers fly on the keyboard, and the room is filled with the sound of her clicking away. We can also hear faint music coming from either Luke's or Lacey's room on the floor above us, punctuated by the tick of a grandfather clock in the foyer. Other than that, the house is silent.

"You have got to be kidding me," says Rita.

"What's the matter?"

"Seven hours and forty-three minutes?"

"For what?"

"To recover the password! To go through all the possible combinations."

"Rita. Oh my God. We don't have that kind of time!"

"No, we don't." She checks her watch.

I'm suddenly afraid that Luke's mom will come purring into the driveway in her Mercedes and get out with several shopping bags. I position myself by the front door so that I can distract her if this happens. Evan follows me.

"What kind of game are you playing here?" he demands. "Do you realize that you're probably breaking all kinds of laws by accessing that laptop? And where did Rita get that Backtrack software anyway? Did she steal it?" His hands are on his hips, and he's wearing an expression of outraged condescension.

"Listen, Evan. I'm not playing any game. I need to know what's happened to my parents and where they are. And don't you even think about taking that tone with me, when you've eavesdropped and forced your way into this situation—"

"Oh, so that means I can't be worried about the possible fallout?"

"Yeah. That's exactly what it means. You don't get to be a priss-pot now."

"Priss-pot?" Evan's mouth works, but oddly enough there's amusement in his eyes, along with irritation.

I don't understand the guy. He's 100 percent annoying, and he's in my way. I push past him and look out the narrow windows to either side of the Carsons' front door.

"Clearly I'm out of my depth among you superspy kids," Evan tosses out. "I'm quite grateful, really, that you let me tag along. Maybe I'll learn a thing or two."

"Maybe," I say shortly, still staring out the window.

"Afraid that Mr. or Mrs. Carson will drive up any moment now?"

"Yes."

"Well, love, priss-pots have their uses. I can stand guard here by the door, if you like."

I turn and evaluate him, try to read the expression in those blue-gray eyes of his. They're looking more blue now. "I like. That would be the first helpful thing you've ever done, Evan."

"Well," Evan says, "when you find your parents, maybe you'll share with our enquiring minds just where the old 'rentals have been and what they've been up to. I can use the material in a screenplay."

"Right—like they talk about that stuff a lot." I don't bother to keep the sarcasm out of my voice.

Evan leans forward, into my space. It makes me uncomfortable, and he takes up too much oxygen. "Ah. But perhaps they keep a Super Spy Journal, love. And you can peruse it using a Super Secret Spy Decoder Ring."

I take two steps backward and stare up into his mocking face. I so wish that I could vaporize it. "You. Are. An. Idiot."

"Why, thank you. I choose to take that as a compliment," he says graciously.

"Proving, without a doubt, that it's true." Very *ungra-ciously*, I turn on my heel and march back to the study in search of Rita, who is much better company.

Evan's soft laughter follows me.

Thirty minutes later, Rita and I still haven't managed to crack Mr. Carson's password, in spite of her trying every combination she can think of off the top of her fashionable head—while Backtrack continues to run. She's tried Luke's birthday, Lacey's birthday, Mrs. Carson's birthday, and even the Carsons' wedding anniversary (the last few conned out of a reluctant Luke). Her eyes are a little manic behind the pink Chanel glasses.

To tell you the truth, I'm starting to feel manic myself. My parents have now been missing for almost forty-eight hours. What if they're being tortured?

I see my dad's face as terrorist thugs kick in his ribs with steel-toed boots, not to mention doing much, much worse. I see my mom hanging from a beam by her bound wrists as she's beaten.

Bile rises in my throat, and I'm hyperventilating before I know it.

Luke has joined us again, in clean clothes with his hair still damp from the shower. He notices my distress before anyone else. "Kari," he says, putting one big, warm hand on each of my shoulders. "Look at me."

I do. I look into his strong-boned face and his concerned brown eyes.

"Take a deep breath: the deepest that you can."

I nod and inhale as much oxygen as I'm capable

of. But I choke on it and start coughing. God forbid I should ever be graceful in front of Luke.

"Kari," he repeats. "I need you to calm down. Okay?"

I gasp, then gasp again.

"Freaking out is not going to help your parents. Or Charlie," he says. "So I need you to center yourself and calm down. Now, deep breath. One."

I do as he tells me.

"Another."

And somehow he gets me focused on just breathing, just being still for a moment or two.

"Don't think," Luke says. "Just focus on taking in that oxygen."

Once I'm breathing normally, I'm torn between being grateful to him and feeling unbelievably stupid. "Thanks," I mutter. I know I'm blushing, because I can feel the heat in my face.

He smiles at me, a warm, genuine, sweet smile that pretty much melts off my toes. "You're welcome."

This moment is incredible. I don't know how to describe it. It feels like a virtual kiss.

Then Rita bangs on Mr. Carson's desk with her fists. She's clearly frustrated that her program is taking so long and she hasn't cracked the password yet.

The moment is gone. And Luke can see that I'm on the verge of getting wound up again. He shakes his finger at me. "Stay calm and focused."

Calm. Focus. Zen.

Now, if I only knew what to do.

Despite growing up the daughter of two spies, despite

a lot of both deliberate and accidental training in the clandestine arena, I have never wanted to be a spy myself. There's no glamour in it if you live it. There's nothing exciting about missing your parents all the time, watching your little brother miss them, and wondering where they are. It's not thrilling to see that Charlie is growing up without them . . . and that they don't even realize it.

Sure, I take it like a marine—what else is there to do? But this is not the life I want for myself. And I try to discourage Rita from viewing it through her rose-colored designer glasses. I guess it's different for her—my parents saved her—but they do their jobs at an enormous cost to their own family.

"Kari, I'm not having any luck," Rita says. "Backtrack will eventually work, but it will take too long." She looks at me as if I have an answer.

Luke looks at me too.

Even know-it-all Evan, who has left his post—big surprise—raises his left eyebrow in a facial question-mark.

It's not like Rita to give up her natural role as leader. But I guess since this involves my parents, it's my battle plan. I wish I knew what to do.

I rack my brain until it cooperates and supplies an idea.

"Where's Lacey's room?" I ask Luke. "I need to borrow something from her."

I follow him up the grand staircase and down a blue-painted hallway hung with gilt-framed antique prints. He points to a white door with a polished brass knob, and I mouth *thanks* at him. I knock.

"What?" Lacey's voice calls rudely, over a Beyoncé song.

"Lacey, it's, uh, Kari. Kari Andrews, from Kennedy Prep?"

"O-kaaay." Her tone is not exactly welcoming. I hear footsteps, and then the door opens. "Dear *God*." She looks me up and down. "Kari, are you really under there? What happened to you? And did you know that, like, *everyone* is looking for you? I'm going to call the cops and claim the reward money, if there is any."

"No! Lacey, look—I know we're not exactly the best of friends, but—"

"OMG, we're not?" She blinks her eyes innocently. "I'm crushed!"

She is *such* a bitch. "Lacey, I need your help. Truly. Honestly. And you can't tell anyone you've seen me."

"Oooooh. What's it worth to you?"

I sigh. "I'll give you a hundred bucks."

"That doesn't even buy a pair of decent sunglasses," she says derisively.

What a chiseler! "Okay, two hundred."

"Deal. So what do you need?"

"Some dark eye shadow."

Lacey casts a glance at my face. "Like you don't have enough on already?"

"Uh . . ."

"Not that you applied it right. What did you do, use a spoon? A house-paint brush? Jeez, Kari, you're hopeless."

"Thanks. Really. You're so sweet." I don't need any

more of this kind of feedback. Sophie teases me about my cosmetic inabilities all the time. Sophie . . . why hasn't she called me back yet?

Lacey points to the vanity stool that's pulled up to a gorgeous, antique dressing table in her room. The walls are papered with eighteenth-century French ladies in gowns, and the whole interior is done in white and gold with pink accents. Why am I not surprised?

"Sit," she says imperiously, like she's the queen and I'm a peasant.

"Why?"

"I'm going to fix your eye makeup," she explains with exaggerated patience.

"Look, Lacey, I don't want your eye shadow for my face," I tell her. "I need it for something else."

She narrows her eyes. "Like what?"

Like none of your bimbo business. "An . . . art project?"

"Puh-lease."

Okay, she's not quite as stupid as she looks. Who knew?

"Kari, I'm wondering just why you're at my house. Probably to make cow eyes at my brother—don't think I haven't noticed that you're hot for him. But that doesn't explain why you'd actually come up the stairs and talk to me, or why you'd try to borrow my makeup when you don't want to learn how to use it like an actual woman might. So why don't you tell me what's going on, before I hit speed dial on my iPhone and call the adorable traffic cop who asked my boobs out on a date after he tore up my speeding ticket." She smiles at me. "He'd probably love a promotion for bringing you in to the station."

Have I mentioned that I really hate Lacey Carson?

"Then you wouldn't get your two hundred bucks," I retort.

She loses her smile and drums her pink fingernails on the dresser. "Info for eye shadow," she says.

Her dad may pull into the driveway at any second. I have no choice, do I?

Chapter Eight

Hearing voices below, Lacey steamrollers her way down the stairs and into her father's study, with me trailing behind her. I've told her the bare minimum, but I had to tell her that. She opens her mouth to say something hateful to Rita—I can tell from the expression on her face—so I try to preempt her.

"Evan, you know Lacey, right?" I say, as if we're at a party or something.

"Socially," he says. "Not yet carnally." His face is the picture of polite as this comes out of his mouth.

I can't help it; a pig snort escapes me before I can stop it.

Lacey's head swivels toward him as if it's a machine gun mounted on a tank. "*What* did you say?"

He grins. "Wax in your ears, love? You heard me."

I have to choke back another pig snort. I may loathe

Evan, but right now I'm silently cheering him. Anyone who takes on Lacey is okay by me.

"In. Your. Dreams." Her tone would freeze the sperm of a killer whale in the arctic, but that doesn't stop her from running her gaze up and down his body. She's clearly intrigued by him but won't admit it. As the Hot Girl, she has to play hard to get.

"Come now," he croons to her. "You never think of me naked?"

She doesn't even bother to look at him. "I never think of you at all."

"Stop harassing my sister, man," Luke tells him, but he's repressing a smile.

"Why? It's fun," Evan points out.

"Why is this ho on my dad's laptop?" Lacey demands, gesturing at Rita.

"Easy, Lace!" Luke says.

"Who are you calling 'ho,' slut?" Rita tosses back.

"Hey," Luke intercedes again. "Dial it down."

"Touching," Evan muses, "that you two girls have such affection for one another."

"Luke!" Lacey snaps. "Why have you let all of these people into Dad's office? He'd be really pissed."

"It's complicated." Luke looks at me, eyebrows raised.

As I'm forced to explain to Lacey just why Rita is on Mr. Carson's computer, Rita narrows her eyes on the belt Lacey is wearing.

"Unbelievable," Rita says. "You? *You're* the one who stole my belt during gym?"

Lacey tosses her hair. "What are you talking about?

Do I look like I need to steal anything? I bought this belt myself at Louis Vuitton."

"Really," Rita says. "What year?"

"Huh?"

"What year?"

"2010," Lacey says, her voice ringing with scorn.

"Yeah? Well that's interesting, since Vuitton didn't make that model until spring 2012, when my mother bought it. You're a liar as well as a thief."

Two spots of red appear high on Lacey's cheeks. "I'd be careful, Larita, real careful what you say, since you're sitting there trying to hack my dad's computer."

"You know what? We don't have time for this," I tell the two of them. I hold out my hand palm up for the eye shadow, and Lacey sullenly gives it to me. Then she adjusts "her" belt.

I take one of her fancy makeup brushes and dust a fine layer of the shadow over Mr. Carson's keyboard. Then I take a deep breath and blow it out, as if trying to extinguish birthday candles. Most of the powder dissipates, but some of it remains stuck to the keys.

"Those," I say, pointing them out, "are the ones that Mr. Carson uses the most."

"Brilliant," Evan says.

"Now we need to come up with combinations of letters and numbers that derive from just these ten or so keys. We're running out of time."

"May I make a suggestion?" Evan asks.

"Like anyone could stop you?" I say.

"We've got to think like Mr. Carson . . . but like Mr. C

trying *not* to think like Mr. C, if you know what I mean."

"Huh?" Lacey rolls her eyes.

"He's the head of the Agency. He's not going to use his dog's name as the password to his computer."

"We don't have a dog," says Lacey.

Evan shoots Luke an expressive look. It asks, *Is she really this stupid?*

"What he means," Rita says acidly, "is that his password is going to be complicated, and probably made up of more symbols and numbers than letters."

Evan nods.

"So let's look at the symbols and numbers that are heaviest in eye shadow," I order them.

"Hel-*lo?*" says Lacey. "Why don't you just try asking me if I know the password?"

We all turn and stare at her as one unit.

"Do you?" Luke demands.

"Well, duh."

"How?" Her brother queries.

She shrugs. "Shoulder surfing."

I'm ready to strangle her. "Why didn't you say so?"

"Because you didn't ask." She smirks. "And besides, you've got little Larita with her gadget . . . so who needs *moi*, the 'dumb blonde'?"

"Little Larita" is poised to spring up and deck the bitch, so I have to hold her back by the seat of her six-hundred-dollar pants.

"Lacey." I take a deep breath. "Please. Nobody thinks you're a dumb blonde. Tell us the password. I'm afraid that someone is going to kill my parents. I'm not kidding."

She evaluates me. "Fine. But you let me in on *every-thing*. No holding back."

I nod.

So, before our disbelieving eyes, Lacey leans forward and types in the password, cool as you please.

Disgusted, Rita removes her thumb drive and shoves it into her pocket.

I move quickly to soothe her. "You would have gotten it too, with your program."

Rita shrugs like it's no big deal, but I can tell she appreciates the credit. She logs on. "I'll run a GREP now and I'll pipe it to the most recently opened documents," she says.

"A who-what?"

"It's a geek thing," Rita says. "You wouldn't understand." And just like that, she re-establishes her superiority over Lacey. Under any other circumstances, I'd have laughed.

We begin to search through recently accessed files. The one we need will have been worked on in the past forty-eight hours, for sure.

I crack my neck nervously as Rita opens and closes several files that have nothing to do with my parents. A car door slams nearby, and we all jump. Luke dashes to the window, but it's a neighbor coming home from work—thank God.

"Got it," Rita announces. Her mouth forms an O as she scans the file, and I crane my neck to see it over her shoulder. We read in utter silence, my eyes flying over phrases such as "unlikely to be coincidental," "dubious timing," and "links to an offshore account held by a shell company."

This doesn't sound good. There's no outright accusation of anything, but there is a recommendation to interrogate, and there are several surveillance reports on subject IA-062192. They're written in dry, boring language and detail a travel schedule that matches my mom's, a dead-drop point, and an acknowledgment that subject IA-062192 "made" her street team and then tried to run.

"IA" can only be Irene Andrews. And "062192" is the date she joined the Agency: June 21, 1992.

Finally, there's a note at the bottom of the document:
SUBJECT IA-062192 IS BEING HELD FOR DEBRIEFING AT LANGLEY.

Rita whistles.

The *Agency* has my mom . . . and they clearly suspect her of something underhanded—which is ridiculous. Making a tail and then losing it, trying to disappear; it's completely normal for my mother. She's on guard all the time. It's part of her job.

And anything to do with an offshore account? That just means that the op she's working on is a black one. One where national security might be compromised if all the details are transparent and trotted out for the media to examine. Think about it: Did the navy write a check and log the specifics when they sent the SEALS into Pakistan to get Osama bin Laden? I don't think so.

"What have you found?" Luke asks.

"The Agency is questioning my mother," I say.

"Where would they detain someone at Langley?"

"Most detaining is probably done in, oh, say . . . a detention center." Evan winks. "However unlikely that may sound."

I ignore him and his idiot sarcasm and look at Luke for guidance.

"He's actually right," he says. "Langley has no *official* detention center. But I've heard rumors of one."

"You don't know where it is?" My tone is urgent.

He shakes his head. "Somewhere in the bowels of the complex."

Once again Lacey shocks us to the core. With a classic hair toss she says, "I know exactly where the detention center is at Langley."

"You do?" Luke stares at her. We all do. Lacey's full of surprises today.

"Of course." She turns and heads for the staircase. "Let's regroup in Luke's room, in case Mom or Dad comes home."

Rita quickly logs out of Mr. Carson's laptop, dusts off the eye shadow from the keyboard, then closes it. We all follow Lacey's perfect, perky buns up the stairs.

"How?" Luke demands. "How do you, of all people, know where the detention center at Langley is?"

She smiles secretively. "Maybe because I've been . . . detained . . . there." She tosses her hair again. "By a totally *hot* security guard."

Luke frowns. "When?"

And Evan is compelled to ask, "Don't these traffic cops and security guards care at all that you're *sixteen*, and therefore what you Yanks like to call jailbait?"

"Not after they get a good look at the girls," Lacey says, gesturing at her biggest assets.

"Slut," Rita mutters under her breath.

Luke looks nauseated.

Evan looks unimpressed.

"So where is this detention center?" I demand.

"Yeah, where?" Rita says. "Let's go!"

Lacey scoffs. "This is the *Agency* we're talking about. We don't just storm the doors and take no prisoners. We need a plan and an official reason to go there."

"What was yours?" Luke presses his sister. "When your security guard buddy showed you the detention center?"

"It's so not important." Lacey waves her hand dismissively.

"Oh, I know what it was. That was the day you got picked up for shoplifting," Luke says. "And you had to spend a little time waiting for Dad to rip you a new one."

"I told you, I did *not* shoplift. I left the store *accidentally* with that handbag, and security jumped to the worst possible conclusion!"

"Uh-huh." Luke skewers her with a glance. "What won't you do to get Dad's attention, Lace?"

"I'm so sure it was accidental," says Rita. "Just like my Vuitton belt *accidentally* fell out of my locker and onto your hips."

Lacey puts her face close to Rita's. "You have no proof of that, and you'd better stop slandering me, or—"

"Or what?" Rita doesn't back up an inch. She doesn't even blink behind the pink Chanel glasses. "Or you'll find your nonexistent receipt from 2010 and staple it to my forehead?"

"That's enough, you two," I say, and shove them apart. "Let's make a plan and go find my mom."

I've been thinking. Just how *do* you break into Langley and make an extraction?

Answer: You don't, especially if you're a group of prep-school kids who will blend into the surroundings about as well as hookers in church. So I figure that we should take advantage of who we are, make it a strength instead of a weakness. What better way to get into Langley than as a tour group from Kennedy Prep, there with our friend Luke, whose dad is the director of the Agency? We'll look so clean-cut and harmless in our navy, white, and plaid uniforms that nobody will ever suspect what we're up to.

But we're going to need the help of another good friend of mine . . . and Rita won't like who it is.

"So," Rita says. "What's your plan?"

"Hang on a sec," I say. "I need to make a call."

Chapter Nine

I go into the bathroom off the hallway with my cell phone and call Kale. Kale Inoue is my other best friend, a senior at Washington High, which is a public school. I met Kale, who is half-Japanese, in my karate class about nine years ago, when my family moved to DC. We were both pretty fast learners, but he was kind of getting a big head because he was beating everyone—until the instructor put him up against me.

While the phone is ringing, I look around the bathroom, which has a claw-foot tub I can picture Thomas Jefferson soaking in and towels with gold fringe and embroidery on them. I go over to the toilet to sit down while I talk, and have to laugh. Even the toilet seat looks like it's made out of mahogany, and instead of a normal flusher thingy there's a gold chain that dangles from a standing rectangular tank. I think maybe Luke's mom has taken this whole antique thing a bit too far.

"Hello?"

"Kale, it's me."

"Mighty Mouse!" he says. "Where you been?"

"It's complicated."

"The entire city's looking for you and Charlie."

"I never called you, by the way."

He gives a low chuckle. "Never."

"Thanks. So, Kale, I really need your help, but I don't want to talk about it on the phone. I need you to meet me right away . . . I'll be in disguise, but you'll know the person with me." I'm probably paranoid, but I wonder if the Agency has bugged my friends' phones? So I tell him to meet me within walking distance of Luke's house but don't give the exact address.

I hang up with Kale and exit the bathroom, only to find Evan standing suspiciously close to the door. Of course he's pretending to look at family photos of the Carsons that are grouped on the hallway wall, but I'm onto him.

"Did you get a good earful?" I ask.

He produces that innocent-as-the-Gerber-baby expression again.

"Don't try to snow me, Evan."

He shrugs. "Okay. So who's Kale?"

"Just because you admit to eavesdropping doesn't mean I'm going to fill you in on anything you might have missed. You have a nerve!"

"Brass bollocks," he says, with a grin. "Want to see them?"

"No, pervert, I do not."

"Is Kale your boyfriend?" Evan asks this just as Luke steps out of his room.

I am mortified, and I almost say no for Luke's benefit, but I refuse to let someone like Evan snoop into my personal life. "That's so none of your business!"

"You might be surprised what *is* my business," he replies with a wink.

Aaargh. Like I asked him? I brush past both of them and go into Luke's room to join the others.

I have to pause for a minute and take in the fact that I am in his inner sanctum. I have dreamed of this moment, though in my fantasy the room looks different and there are filmy white curtains blowing in a beach breeze and Luke and I are, um, wearing a lot less.

But back to reality. The decor is basically nautical, with a lot of navy and yellow, but I'm guessing that Luke stopped his mother before she went off the rails and ordered him a custom-made sailboat bed or anything. Between the windows, mounted on the wall over his bed, there is a very cool model of a tall ship with all the rigging and sails. I wonder if he put it together.

Over his antique rolltop desk there's a trophy case that holds all of his track awards. I try really hard not to look at the bed, because it embarrasses me. And why am I even thinking about it when my mom is locked up at the Agency, and my dad is who knows where? That's awful. What kind of person am I?

I pull myself together, clear my throat, and tell them all about my tentative plan to go into the Agency tomorrow, in our uniforms, as a tour group from Kennedy Prep.

"I think that might work," Luke says, nodding.

"Have you lost your minds?" Evan asks, looking scandalized.

"I'll change my regulation skirt for a shorter one," Lacey says. At her brother's disgusted look, she throws up her hands. "What? We might need me to distract somebody."

Rita practically gags herself on Luke's bedpost.

"I'm going to go meet my friend Kale a couple of blocks away and bring him back here," I confess, wincing as Rita's head comes up and she glares at me.

"*Kale?* You have got to be kidding me. Why?"

"Rita, give me a break. We need him." I turn and walk downstairs again and out the front door. She follows me like an angry dog after a mailman.

"We do not need him! He's a pain in the ass," she says.

I drag a hand down my face and look for the best angle to take with her. For some reason Rita can't stand Kale, and the feeling is mutual. Maybe it's because Kale doesn't have any patience with her bent for up-market fashion and thinks she's a snob, on top of being a know-it-all. Or maybe it's because Rita thinks he's got a chip on his shoulder about anyone who's not working class. Personally, I think if they'd stop bickering long enough to get to know each other, they might get along. But there doesn't seem to be any chance of that.

"Rita, we all know you're the brains behind this operation," I tell her, deciding that flattery is a good way to go. "But we need some more muscle, just in case we get into trouble."

"We have Luke and Evan for that. Besides, Kale is a short dude."

I turn to look at her, my eyebrows raised. "Do you have any idea what that 'short dude' can do? I guarantee you that he could take down Luke and Evan, both, before they even knew what was happening."

I break off because we've reached the address I gave Kale, and like clockwork he turns the corner onto the street we're on. He's always punctual.

Rita curls her lip and turns away.

Kale, who was wearing his simple, uncomplicated smile a second ago, spots her and scowls as he approaches. "What's the brat doing here?"

"What's the grease monkey doing here?" Rita retorts.

Kale has completely rebuilt a 1972 Mustang over the past four years, using salvage parts as he can find them. "Hey, at least I can fix my own car, unlike you, princess."

"You only call me that because you're jealous."

"That would be '*envious*,' Miss Prep School Education. 'Jealous' would require that I had feelings for you. And, no, I don't think so. I'm happy to stand on my own two feet, learning from my dad instead of living off him."

"Yeah?" Rita says. "Well maybe your dad's around more than mine." There are blotches of pink across her cheeks as she unzips her Prada messenger bag and digs for something inside. Something that I'm sure she doesn't need.

"Poor little rich girl." Kale shoves his hands into his pockets and then has the grace to look sheepish as Rita hisses in a breath.

"Screw you," she says.

"Okay, that's enough!" I am going to lose my mind if I have to play referee between Rita and Kale *and* between Rita and Lacey. "Do not make me tape your mouths closed."

"You try that and see how it works out for you," Kale challenges me.

"Hey, I smoked you in our last karate class," I remind him. I drop my voice, even though there's nobody around and it's not as if the trees are bugged. "But forget about that. Kale, you're here because we need you to help us find my mom, who's locked up in some detention center at Langley. We have to break her out."

Kale stares at me. "Say again?"

"My mom and dad work for the Agency, Kale. They're spies."

I give him a moment to absorb this.

"Okay . . . ," he says slowly.

"Some brain stem there thinks my mom is taking bribes or something—I don't know, it's hard to tell—and we have to find her so that she can get out and uncover whatever plot there may be to bring her down. I'm guessing here. But my dad is missing too, and she's probably the only one who knows where *he* is."

"You're crazy," Kale informs me. "Why don't you just sit tight and let the Agency ask their questions, so she can prove how dumb they are? And then she can walk out on her own."

"Look, normally I'd say you're right. But some really strange things have been going on." I fill him in on the Code Black messages from my parents and then the attempted kidnapping by Mitch and Gary Gray Suit in the park.

"And those guys work for the Agency," I emphasize. "Why would they try to grab me? And then why would they put out the word with the cops and the media that Charlie and I are missing children? None of this is adding up."

Kale nods. He's actually very good-looking, with that golden-olive skin of his and beautiful, upturned dark eyes. His hair is cut with a razor and I think it looks cool, even if Rita doesn't.

Speaking of Rita, I notice that she's been covertly looking at Kale's body, as if she's never noticed it before. I bite down on my lip so I don't smirk at her.

"So let me get this straight," he says. "People from the Agency are trying to kidnap you . . . and you've decided to just walk right into the hornet's nest and make it easy for them?"

Kale does have a point. "I'll go in disguise," I tell him.

"As Goth girl? Like you are now, but in a Kennedy Prep uniform?"

I realize that won't fly, since Kennedy has a strict grooming policy. Lacey will have to help me change my look yet again. I shudder at the thought of putting myself into her long pink claws, but there's really no alternative, is there?

We walk back to Luke's house and ring the bell. I introduce Kale to everyone and we head back upstairs, while he looks around at the house with something close to awe. Kale's dad is a cop, and his mom took off on them a few years back, so they live in a utilitarian apartment pretty close to his high school.

"Don't get any grease on the banister," Rita says to him.

"Don't get any snot on it either, brat." He gives it right back to her.

Evan's eyebrows shoot up, and he looks from one to the other, amused.

"Just saying. You probably don't come into many houses like this, do you, Kale?"

Wow. Rita's out of control today.

But I don't need to worry about Kale and self-defense. "No, Rita. But you and your spoiled attitude have probably been thrown out of a lot of them."

She flushes hot pink. She knows when she's been beaten.

Poor Luke is speechless.

Unlike Evan. "Maybe we should put these two in a guest bedroom for a while, just to work out all their sexual tension."

Kale spins on his heel and punches him in the bicep.

Evan rubs at his arm. "Shite, man. You don't hold anything back, do you?" Then he gasps as Rita slams him in his shoulder. "Why the violence, when all I did was point out the obvious?"

"Okay, people!" I raise my voice. "I need everyone to stop messing around and focus. Do you understand?"

"Aye, aye, Cap'n Kari," says Luke, with a small salute and a quirk of his lips. "May I offer you a seat?" He gestures toward his bed.

I swallow hard as I ease myself down onto his mattress. "Thanks."

As he looks at me on his bed, the quirk at the corner

of his mouth grows into a full-fledged smile, with something just a little wicked hidden under it.

Oh. My. God. I'm going to melt into a puddle if he does that again. I take a deep breath and avoid his gaze.

Then the moment is ruined as Evan bounces onto the bed right beside me, hard, so that I bounce too, and almost end up in his lap. Is it my imagination, or does Luke look a little annoyed?

I untangle myself from Evan, who peers down at me provocatively. One of these days I'm going to tell him that he is *not* God's gift to women, as he seems to think. He's more like a curse.

"So, what's the drill?" Kale stands with his hands on his hips, deliberately with his back to Rita.

"Luke," I say, "do you have an old Kennedy Prep uniform that Kale can wear?"

"Yeah." He scans Kale, sizing him up. "But the pants'll be too long."

"Lacey?" I call.

"What?" she calls back, from her room.

"Can you sew?"

"Are you *high*?"

"That's what I thought."

"I can," Rita says.

Kale's eyebrows crawl into his razor-cut hair.

"I alter my mom's clothes to fit me," she says, by way of explanation.

"Could you hem a pair of Luke's khakis to fit Kale?"

She's silent for a moment. "Yes," she says. "If he's grateful."

Kale shoots her a death stare.

Evan guffaws like some kind of backward British donkey.

"What—do you want me to kiss your feet, princess?" Kale says.

"Forget it!" I yell. "Luke, we just need some duct tape. These two can't get near each other or they'll—"

"Shag," Evan says.

"Kill each other!" I finish. I push him, and he falls off Luke's bed, laughing.

"Yeah. Duct tape," says Luke, and dives out of the room, snorting with laughter.

Rita hurls herself over the bed and sits on Evan. "One more word out of you, and I will kill you, Brit Boy," she warns him.

Kale inhales softly as he checks out Rita's backside while she sits astride Evan, who is laughing like a loon.

"God, I love a violent woman!" he gasps.

"Apologize," she orders him.

"I think not."

"Give it a rest, brat," Kale says. He walks over, leans forward, and loops an arm around Rita's waist, lifting her off Evan as effortlessly as if she were a Polly Pocket doll.

"Don't abuse the help," he says, setting her on her feet.

Rita turns fuchsia. Seriously, so pink that her skin matches the Chanel eyeglasses.

"What did I bloody tell you all?" Evan demands. "They're *so* going to shag!"

Rita tries to fall on him and kill him, but Kale intercepts her once again. She hangs in the air from the "short dude's" grip, arms and legs flailing in disbelief.

Then Kale sets her down without a word.

Rita is weirdly speechless herself. I'm not sure I've ever seen her that way.

Both of them stay quiet as Luke, Lacey, and I work out a plan to infiltrate Langley tomorrow afternoon. Evan periodically breaks in to say that we are all "barking mad" and that we can't be serious.

"Shut up, Evan!" I snap at him, after his third interruption. "You weren't invited, but you've insisted on being here. Now, are you in or are you out?"

He gives me a level stare. He plays with the change in his pocket for a moment, stalling. "Bloody hell," he says. "I'm going to regret this. . . ."

I raise my eyebrows at him and wait.

"I'm in," he says with a sigh.

It's at this moment that we hear a car door slam.

"Oh, shit!" Luke exclaims. "Yeah, you're in now, buddy—because one of my parents is home."

Lacey runs to the window. "It's Mom," she says.

We hear the *clip-clop clip-clop* of Mrs. Carson's high heels as she approaches the front door.

"Run, everybody!" Luke orders. "Down the stairs, then straight back to the kitchen. Sneak out through the yard. I'm going to distract her. As soon as she's inside the house, sprint to my Jeep." He digs the keys out of his pocket and tosses them to me. "I'll meet you out there."

We practically dive down the stairs and scurry like rats, one after the other, down the hallway as Luke opens the door a crack and blocks it with his body.

"Hey, Mom! How was your day?"

"Hello, sweetheart. Fine, thanks. And yours?"

"Great, great. I think I aced that chemistry exam."

"Wonderful. Honey, you wouldn't know anything about a three-hundred-and-fifty-dollar charge on my Bloomingdale's account, would you?"

"No . . ."

"Then I'll need to speak to your sister. Again."

"Oh. Um, I don't think she's home."

"Her car's in the driveway—Lucas, please move aside so I can get in the door. Here, take this bag for me, will you?"

The kitchen door closes behind the last of us, Kale, as she says these words. We sprint across the backyard, crouching low and keeping along the bushes. Lacey opens the gate noiselessly and we hug the exterior wall closely as we stream through. She latches the gate behind us, and we all scramble, bent double, into the front yard and then finally make it to Luke's Jeep.

"Don't press the fob to unlock it," hisses Lacey. "It'll make a noise."

I nod and insert the key into the driver's-side door the old-fashioned way. Then I press the button inside that will unlock all the doors at once.

We all clamber in and slide over, keeping our heads ducked. Kale goes into the back cargo area and lies flat. My heart is beating triple time, even though there's no way Mrs. C. will recognize me dressed like this.

The four of us wait, breathing heavily, for Luke to come out.

And then things get worse.

Another car pulls into the driveway, and this one can only be Mr. Carson's. We squash down onto the floor like sardines and just pray.

A car door opens, then closes. We hear the crackle of grocery bags. Feet, men's feet, clop along the driveway, then up the front walkway and to the house. The heavy front door opens, then closes.

We wait some more.

Lacey's cell phone begins to ring. She pulls it out to look at the caller ID. "My dad," she whispers. She puts it on vibrate.

We continue to wait.

And finally, at long last, the front door opens and closes yet again, and lighter male footsteps approach the Jeep.

"Miss me?" asks Luke, as he opens the driver's-side door and climbs in.

I exhale in relief.

I've left the keys in the ignition for him, and he starts the Jeep and backs out of the driveway. "What did you charge on Mom's Bloomie's account, Lace?"

"Nothing," she says from the backseat.

"Well, it was an expensive nothing, then," says Luke, his voice resigned. "She's pissed, and she's looking for you."

"Whatever," Lacey says, sullenly.

I hope that by tomorrow evening Mr. Carson isn't going to be even more pissed than his wife. And looking for *all* of us.

Chapter Ten

"I told Mom and Dad I have a study group tonight for physics," Luke says, as he drives us away from his house and into the gathering darkness. "Lacey, I told them I didn't know where you were, but you might be at an aerobics class with your phone in a locker."

"Good thinking," his sister says. "I knew I kept you around for some reason."

Luke turns his head slightly and asks, "Kari, where do you need to go?"

I exhale. "It's a little complicated. I have to get back to the Comfort Inn where Charlie is, but we also have to move tonight. And I can't go back in looking like a Goth girl, because a guy from the Agency spotted me this morning."

There's a long silence.

"I wish we'd had time to borrow some clothes of my mom's," Luke says.

"We can use some of *my* mom's," Rita volunteers. "If you'll take me back to my car at Kennedy Prep, then I can drive home, get the stuff, and meet you somewhere."

"Don't you live in Georgetown?" Lacey asks. "Isn't it easier if we just stop at a mall and buy her something?"

I open my mouth to say that I don't have any money, and then realize that's not true. I have the credit cards and cash from the Union Station locker. "Lacey's right. Let's just buy an outfit somewhere—we have a couple of hours until the stores close. But I'll have to stay in the car. I can't take the risk of being seen. Rita, I'll give you a credit card."

"I'm great at shopping," says Lacey. "I'll be happy to run in and pick something for you."

Rita snorts, loudly.

"Do *not* give my sister your credit card," Luke says.

"Hey!" Lacey smacks him. "What are you trying to say?"

"You know exactly what."

Rita sniffs. "Like she needs a credit card to shoplift?"

Lacey glares at her. "Look, bitch—"

"Enough!" Evan shouts. "*I* will go in and get Kari something."

"You?" Rita eyes him. "What would you know about women's clothing?"

"Quite a bit, actually. Especially how to take it off."

Silence ensues, then Kale starts to laugh. "Where did you find this guy?"

"He found us," I say sourly.

Luke pulls into the parking lot of a local shopping

mall and right up to the front door of Macy's. "Knock yourself out, Evan."

"He doesn't know what sizes to get!" Rita struggles with her seat belt.

"Really? I'd say Kari's a women's size four, with a thirty-two A bust. Am I right, love?" Evan calls the question from the backseat.

I'm utterly mortified that he's guessed my tiny bra size and announced it in front of Luke. I could kill him, with my bare hands. "B," I lie.

Evan gets out of the Jeep and stretches his long legs. He leans back in and runs his eyes over what he can see of my body. After too long a pause and a quick glance at Luke, he repeats, "Thirty-two B. Of course. What was I thinking?"

He closes the door and saunters toward the brightly lit doors of Macy's before I can even offer him cash or a credit card. I hope he falls down the escalators. Or gets brained by a toppling mannequin. Or rips his pants on a nail and gets arrested for public indecency . . .

Evan returns with a boxy little houndstooth suit in black and white, serviceable black bag and pumps, black pantyhose, black reading glasses, and a big hair clip. He also hands me a small Victoria's Secret bag containing a lacy, electric-violet bra and panty set. The panties are a size small. The bra is a thirty-two A.

He winks and smiles knowingly as I check the size on it.

I grit my teeth and force myself to ask politely how much I owe him.

"On the house, love," is all he says.

"I can't let you—" I begin.

"When are you taking *me* shopping, lover-boy?" Lacey asks.

He chuckles and wags a finger at her.

Now all I need is a place to de-Goth and go corporate.

We pick a McDonald's bathroom as the perfect changing spot. I dive down the access hallway, which is two steps inside the door, and start by scrubbing all the makeup off my face. Larita comes in with me and provides a bright pink lipstick and some blush.

Soon all the garish Goth is rinsed away and the new "execu-me" emerges. I look like an office manager or executive assistant, and nobody would ever guess that I'm toting electric-violet, lacy lingerie in my handbag.

I can walk into the Comfort Inn now, lead out my little girl Charlotte by the hand, and nobody will look closely enough to tell me apart from the thousands of other office workers in DC.

That's exactly what I do, while Luke and the others wait outside, even though Kale is probably getting sick of lying scrunched up in the cargo space. Then we drive to a Best Western closer to Luke's house in Great Falls.

I swap out my ID and credit cards quickly for new ones from the Union Station backpack.

We all agree to meet at Luke's the next day at around two p.m. That will give us time to change, get our gear ready, and get to Langley by late afternoon. Mr. Carson is usually tied up in meetings then, so there's little risk of us running into him.

Charlie and I check in to the hotel without incident and—thank God—with no sign of Mitch and company.

The next day I don't want to chance stealing a car from the Best Western parking lot. So I ask the hotel to call for a Yellow Cab to take us to Luke's. Meanwhile, I put on the violet lingerie, the junior executive suit and heels, plop the glasses onto my nose, and totally screw up my attempt at makeup.

I can hear Sophie laughing at me as I cuss and wipe off the smeared eyeliner with a damp washcloth, only to start again. Why hasn't Sophie called me back? It's really starting to bother me.

I finally give up on the stupid eye makeup and just do my best with lipstick and blusher. The glasses will hide my eyes, right?

Charlie grouses about having to be Charlotte again, and I feel bad for him. I reason that we're only going straight in a cab to Luke's house, and then he'll be changing anyway, so I let him dress in his normal clothes. "Just take off your glasses, kiddo, and put on your baseball cap."

He nods, and we take the elevator downstairs from our room on the fourth floor. My prop glasses are filthy, and I take them off to clean them with a tissue from Rita's purse.

The doors open on the ground floor with a *ding* and we get off. Too late I see a young cop standing in the lobby, chatting with a hotel employee. I freeze, glasses in hand. He looks over at us casually, and I jam the glasses onto my nose and drag Charlie quickly past him.

We're almost to the doors, and I can see the Yellow Cab turning into the circular drive when the policeman calls, "Excuse me, miss?"

I squeeze Charlie's hand more tightly and hustle out the door.

"Miss! Hold up there!"

A quick glance over my shoulder reveals that he's coming after us.

The cab pulls up.

"I need to ask you a couple of questions, please," the cop says.

We haul ass to the cab, and I wrench open the door. "Get in!" I tell Charlie.

"Can't, sorry, we're late for an appointment," I tell the officer, and jump into the backseat with my brother.

"Hey!" yells the cop.

"*Go*," I say urgently to the taxi driver, a hunched old guy in a tweed cap. I give him an address three blocks from Luke's house, and without hesitation, he puts the pedal to the metal.

Only as we turn into traffic do I realize that the cabby isn't old at all.

He's Mitch.

He presses the power lock button, and the adrenaline that rushed through my body at the sight of the cop freezes cold.

"Hiya, kids," Mitch says with a nasty grin. "How've you been?"

This is not happening.

Except it is.

And I have to figure out what to do.

Charlie's eyes are wide and stricken. I squeeze his hand to reassure him.

"How did you find us?" I demand of Mitch.

"Wouldn't you like to know."

"You must want to go to jail for kidnapping."

He scoffs. "Not gonna happen, sweetheart. This is Agency business."

Mitch has locked the doors, so jumping out of the car isn't an option. We don't have a gun to put to his head, unfortunately. And we're not filthy rich enough to bribe him.

"Last time I checked, the Agency has to operate under U.S. law, Mitch."

"We're covered on this," he assures me.

Well, isn't that interesting.

I take stock of the vehicle. The cab is an older model that doesn't have a partition separating the front and back seats. This makes Mitch more vulnerable than he thinks he is.

However, I don't have Mace in Rita's bag. I don't have a stun gun.

What do I have?

A small can of hairspray. A set of house keys. And . . . I think fast. And Charlie's backpack.

"You sure about that?" I ask, as I slide the little can of spray out of my purse. I pass it to Charlie and touch my index and middle finger to my eyes. Then I mouth, *One, two, three.*

"Yeah, as a matter of fact, I am, Karina." Mitch's tone is loathsome and condescending. We pull up at a light.

There's no car next to us. No car behind us. Nobody to see.

One, I mouth at Charlie.

Two. Three!

Charlie pops over the front seat and depresses the nozzle on the hairspray, hosing Mitch right in the eyes.

"Goddamn it!" he screams.

I loop the strap of Charlie's backpack over Mitch's head before he can get his hands off the wheel and up to his face. Then I twist the whole pack and pull it tight so that I have Mitch garroted.

I twist the pack again and wedge the straps under the headrest for extra strength, as Mitch cusses, flails, and tries alternately to wipe his eyes, grab me, or get his fingers under the strap around his neck. But I've made sure he can't.

"Drive, Mitch," I say in a sweet voice. "Open your eyes, put your hands on the wheel and drive us where I tell you to go."

He gags and claws again at the strap around his throat. "I can't see!"

"Do it!" I order. I pull a bottle of water out of Rita's purse, twist off the cap and dash some in his eyes. "The light is green. Go."

"And if I don't?" he challenges, even though he can barely speak.

Maybe I'll just ram my house keys through your jugular."

"You're bluffing."

"No, Mitch, I'm not," I lie. "You're really starting to

piss me off, and you don't want to piss off a sociopath like me."

A car has driven up behind us, and it honks.

"Drive, asshole!" I shriek into his ear.

So Mitch drives.

As a tiny reward, I loosen my grip on the strap enough to let him have a few molecules of oxygen.

I direct him to the McDonald's where I changed disguises last night. I make him park. And then I knock him out manually at two pressure points on his throat. He won't be out long, but it'll be long enough for us to get away.

I make sure that Mitch's collar is turned up so that nobody can see that he's tied by the throat to the headrest. I adjust his hat to a jaunty angle.

Charlie cleans his stuff out of the backpack, we dump it into my purse, and we get out of the car—to all appearances calm and cool.

Nobody waiting in the drive-through line notices that I'm shaking like Jell-O in an earthquake or that my badly lipsticked smile is pasted on.

We walk into the McDonald's. The ladies' room is occupied, so we go into the men's and lock the door. I have to ask Charlie to dial Kale's cell phone number because my hands are trembling so much, and when he hands the phone to me, my voice comes out in a squeak.

"Mighty Mouse? That you?"

"Kale. This is an emergency. Come pick Charlie and me up behind the Pep Boys at the corner of . . ." I give him quick directions. My brother and I exit the men's room and walk out the other side of the McDonald's. We walk a block over to the Pep Boys and hide behind a vending machine, praying that Mitch will stay unconscious or at least tethered until long after Kale picks us up.

Chapter Eleven

We're an hour late by the time we get to Luke's house. Charlie and I have been riding flat on the floor of Kale's car with a couple of jackets thrown over us. It's filthy and smells like fried fish. Kale has a thing for Long John Silver's.

Despite the crick in my neck and the less-than-comfortable conditions, I'm thankful for Kale's friendship and our freedom.

Luke's parents have gone to a charity benefit, so we have a couple of hours to change and go over our plans for "storming" Langley.

Kale pulls into the circular driveway to let Charlie and me out of the car. He's going to park a couple of blocks away and walk back.

We ring the doorbell, and Lacey appears to let us in. Her hair is teased to awesome proportions, her white oxford shirt unbuttoned invitingly and tied tightly at the waist. Then there's the skirt—if it can still be called that. It's more like a small napkin, the pleats gasping for decency.

Her lips are shiny and her eyes are avid, dying for adventure. "You're late," she says. "Everyone else has been here for over an hour."

"Yeah, well." I don't tell her about our little problem with being kidnapped. "You look . . . incredible. And I'm going to need your help."

"Well, duh," she retorts, scanning me up and down.

We follow her inside and up the stairs.

Rita and Evan are hanging out in Luke's room, already in uniform. Luke is tying his tie. Rita's researching something on her iPad.

"Look who's fashionably late," she says. "What took you guys so long?"

Evan raises his eyebrows as he takes in the rumpled state of my suit and the carpet fibers from Kale's car stuck all over my black pantyhose. "Did you *roll* here?"

Only Luke notices that my knees are trembling and that my hands aren't quite steady. "Kari? What happened?" He leaves the ends of his tie dangling and walks over to me. He puts his hands on my shoulders and looks down into my face. "You okay?"

"Yeah," I say.

"No," Charlie states baldly.

Luke steers me gently toward his bed, and I sit down. Everyone stares at me.

"We got kidnapped," Charlie announces. "Cab-napped, to be exact."

I briefly summarize what happened.

Rita cheers.

Evan guffaws. "Bollocks," he says. "Good story, though . . ."

Luke is still staring at me with his mouth slightly open. "You strangled the guy with the straps of Charlie's backpack?"

"One strap," I correct him. I glare at Evan. "It's *not* bollocks."

"Did you get his wallet?" Lacey wants to know.

"Did you really just ask me that?"

"Yeah. Because he might have had an ID card to get into Langley." She puts her hands on her hips and shakes her head. "You're hopeless." She checks her watch. "And we need to get you dressed, so come with me."

I tell Charlie to change into his Madison uniform, and then follow Lacey down the hall to her room.

First she outfits me in one of her own Kennedy uniforms—plaid skirt, white shirt, knee socks. Then she tells me once again to sit my "skinny ass" down on her vanity stool. This time I follow orders and put myself into the pink claws of Satanic Barbie.

Lacey turns my stool to face her. She frowns at me, drums an index finger on her lip, and walks around me, evaluating her raw material. I feel *very* raw under her scrutiny. Pretty much like a package of pork, three days past its sell-by date.

"We'll start with the hair," she says. "We can't change the Kennedy uniform much, but . . . wait." She smirks and gets a small, square goose-down pillow from her bed.

"We *can* change your body. Stand up and undo the waist-band of your skirt."

"Uh. Why do I have to be fat?"

"Because we have to make you look different," she says reasonably.

I follow orders. She untucks my borrowed white uni-form shirt and stuffs the pillow up under it. Somehow she manages to button the waistband of the pleated plaid skirt around everything, then stands back to look.

"Beautiful," she says.

I try to turn so that I can see too.

"Nope. No peeking until I'm done."

Next, Lacey does horrible things to my hair. She squirts it with stuff, teases it, and clips it back from either side of my face with two barrettes—a style that even I know hasn't been popular since . . . when? The year I was born?

Is she trying deliberately to make me look fat and dorky around her brother?

Probably.

Lacey pulls up her desk chair for the makeup job. For some reason this involves crumpling up a tiny piece of paper and sticking it under one of those small circular Band-Aids, right in the middle of my forehead, but just off center.

"Lacey—"

"Shhhh. Quiet. Don't speak in the presence of genius," she says. She applies a thick foundation to my face—not a shade that matches my skin—and works it in especially over the round Band-Aid. She adds powder and then more foundation.

She adds a final layer of powder to my forehead and then, of all things, dabs a tiny amount of lip gloss up there, rubbing it around the edges of the Band-Aid. What is this sick Susie-Q doing to me?

I try not to squirm as she breaks out the brow liner and eye pencils next and makes strange additions over my eyes.

I continue to sit there, and she scares me next with a liver-colored lipstick that I wouldn't put on the wrong end of a dog.

"Oh yeah," Lacey says, nodding as she steps back and evaluates me. "Now, for the grand finale." She fishes around in her closet and comes out with the most horrific, beat-up, unisex camping shoes I've ever seen. "Put those on."

"Do I have to?"

"Yes."

I do. I stand up.

She laughs and laughs. Then she laughs some more.

I turn slowly to face her mirror and gape. I am a pot-bellied pygmy with scary, 1970s hair that looks like a grown-out bad perm. I have a giant, pulsing zit on my forehead. It's red, infected, and shiny with oil. My eyebrows are thick as caterpillars, and they almost meet over my nose.

I have dark circles under my eyes, my mouth looks like a dab of liverwurst, and fine, penciled "hairs" adorn my upper lip.

Lacey is still howling as Rita walks into the room. She takes one look at me and blanches.

"*Why* did you let her do that to you?"

I'm still fixated, appalled, on the Frisbee-size "zit" in the middle of my forehead. "I wasn't exactly aware— wasn't facing the mirror."

"Did I invite Rita in here?" Lacey demands, after gasping for breath.

We ignore her.

"Get out!" she says, popping a piece of bubble gum into her mouth.

"Well, one thing is for sure," Rita says. "Not even your own mother will recognize you."

"Thank God." I'm starting to realize that, though I look like a complete troll, the disguise is a brilliant one. Lacey may be a bitch, but she's talented.

"You're going to scare Charlie."

"Probably."

"Are you people deaf?" Lacey calls. "You are invited to get the hell out of my room, now."

"Thanks, Lace. You've done wonders. We're leaving."

She blows a bubble and pops it. "Yep. I should charge for my work."

I already owe her two hundred dollars. Isn't that enough?

A last glance into her mirror makes me wince. I so do not want Luke to see me looking like this. . . .

But I don't have a choice. As I step out of Lacey's room, he steps out of his.

Luke scans me from head to toe and just blinks. "Holy cow," he says. "Is that you, Kari?"

I make a strangled noise in the affirmative.

He blinks again. "*Damn.*"

"What can I say?" I ask dryly. Inside, I'm dying a slow death that he's witnessing this. I will never live it down.

But at this point I may as well make the best of it—and hope it helps get me into Langley unnoticed. "Your sister's a magician."

He shakes his head. "That doesn't make her a nice person." He, too, is fixated on the zit. He grimaces. "How'd she do that?"

I shrug.

He's still unable to tear his horrified gaze from it when Evan and Kale—who arrived and dressed in a uniform of Luke's during my transformation—come out of his room. They, too, gawk at me.

"Christ! What a horror show." Evan peers at the zit.

"I'm going to start charging admission," I say.

Kale looks away, then can't help himself. He glances again.

"I'm sure you're going to tell me that my pimple isn't that big," I say conversationally.

"Are you joking?" Evan asks. "It's the size of a pie."

Rita snorts. "Big as a circus ring."

"More like an asteroid," says Kale.

"You people are great for a girl's self-esteem," I tell them.

Charlie emerges from Luke's room to check me out too. He claps a hand over his mouth and giggles uncontrollably. Wow. There's no loyalty in this world, is there?

I will think about getting revenge on Lacey some other

day. Right now I want to find my mother. "Can we go now?"

"Sure thing," Luke says.

"Charlie?" I query. "Rita? You guys have all the equipment for dealing with the security cameras, right?"

"Check." Rita smiles with satisfaction. "I have a gadget you're going to love."

"What kind of gadget?" Evan asks with suspicion. "Is it legal?"

"Yes and no," Rita says. "Depending on how you use it."

"I don't like the sound of that," he says. He folds his arms over his chest. "In fact, I still think you're all crazy to even attempt this Langley escapade. I'm not at all sure I'm going with you—"

"You're pussing out, Brit Boy?" Rita jibes. "Don't have the stomach for it?"

Evan's expression is hard to read. He's half irritated . . . but again, I see a trace of amusement. Maybe it's just his English "superiority" to us Yanks.

Whatever it is, it makes me want to deck him. "You are unbelievable," I say. "You sneak and eavesdrop and blackmail your way into this, and now you want to back out?" I poke him in the chest. "Unacceptable. You said you were in."

His eyes glint oddly as he looks down at me. "Fine. I succumb to the peer pressure. I'll toddle along to Langley with you. I've never been arrested . . . there's a first time for everything, I suppose."

I make a noise of contempt.

Evan bursts out laughing.

"What are you laughing at, you . . . you . . . jackass?!"

"You," he says. "You look so ridiculously ugly—" He gasps for breath.

Luke steps between us before I can hit him. "She's a very good sport about it," he says quietly. Soothingly.

I inhale the scent of his freshly laundered shirt and a sporty, breezy aftershave. I forget about being mad at Evan, because I could stand there and breathe in the delicious smell of Luke all day. He's standing close enough that I can feel his body heat. I look up into his eyes, trying to keep the longing out of my own.

Then I remember what I look like—a troll from under a bridge—and I step away, pull myself together. "Charlie, you have the laser pointers? The comm units?"

He nods.

"Rita, you brought the extra Kennedy lapel pins and the little Velcro dots?"

She nods.

"Kale, you brought your A-game?"

He gives me a thumbs-up.

"And Luke . . . you'll keep your sister under control?"

He snorts.

"I heard that!" Lacey says, coming out of her room with her Vuitton purse slung over her arm.

Evan's lips twitch. "Louis and his logos will come in handy at Langley, I'm sure."

Lacey tosses her hair over her shoulder. "A girl needs her accessories."

"And those of others," Rita mutters under her breath.

We're a strange and motley crew, but we're on a mission: to find my mom and break her out.

Chapter Twelve

By five p.m. we're en route to Langley. Charlie breaks out the comm units that were in our Union Station backpacks. They're tiny, and we attach them to the backs of gold Kennedy Prep pins that have the school crest on them. Then everyone puts one on the lapel of his or her uniform jacket.

Charlie and Rita will stay in the back of Luke's Jeep, monitoring the situation with the laptop, which will keep track of our comm units. Rita should also be able to hack into the CCTV system and keep a lookout for us.

We pull up to the security booth, Luke at the wheel, and he shows the guard his ID and tells him that he's bringing in a tour group. We all wave like clean-cut, preppy, plaid-accessorized angels.

Angels or not, we are all required to hand over picture IDs before Luke can move forward another inch, and the vehicle is scanned, inside and out, for possible weapons or explosives. Evan jokes that we only have Lacey the Sex Bomb with us, but the security guys do not find that funny. Lacey smiles and takes it as a compliment.

I just pray that Charlie's fake ID and mine pass inspection. I am masquerading as Louise Snodgrass, and Charlie is Patrick McMahon. Thank God, the guards don't have any issue with them. The interior of the car is dark, and the guards aren't all that worried about a group of prep-school kids. Finally we are admitted to the grounds.

Langley isn't just one building. It's a vast, sprawling campus that encompasses the Original Headquarters Building, the New Headquarters Building, an auditorium, research facilities, memorials, parks, and training grounds.

Luke parks his Jeep in the designated area, and Charlie and Rita stay in the back cargo area, hidden by the tinted windows.

Luke, Lacey, Evan, Kale, and I get out and walk in through the doors of the New Headquarters Building, which is huge, white, and modern, with an impressive arch of skylights. Here we have to stop to go through more security and get visitor passes.

Luke and his sister know the guards on duty, since they've been here to visit their dad.

"Hey, Richie," Luke says, casually. "How's Martha? The kids?"

"Good, good. Thanks for asking. How're you, Luke?"

"Can't complain." Luke slips off his watch, empties his pockets of change, and drops all of his metal into a plastic bowl. He adds his phone and turns to the other man working at the counter by the metal detectors as he walks through. "How about you, Jake?"

"Same old, same old," Jake says. "Had me a hot date last Saturday, though."

"She a keeper?"

"Too early to tell, my man." Jake hands Luke the plastic bowl and nods more formally to Lacey. "Hello, young lady."

"Hey, Jake," she says coolly. She puts her palm flat on his chest and stands on tiptoe to kiss his cheek.

Looking stunned, he watches her sashay through the metal detector and get her purse on the other side. He and Richie exchange a quick glance; Jake shakes his head.

Luke ignores his sister's shenanigans and snaps his watch back around his wrist. "Guys, these are my friends Ka—ah, Louise, Evan, and Kale. We're going to give them the grand tour after we meet up with Dad. It's for our government class."

The guards nod.

"This whole tour was actually his idea." Lacey delivers this lie so easily that I'd believe it myself if I didn't know better.

"We'll just wait in his office, if that's all right," Luke says.

The guards look at each other, then shrug. "Yeah, okay." Clearly, they know the Carson kids well.

I don't have a purse on me, so I drop my charm bracelet, Kennedy Prep pin, phone, and watch into a plastic bowl. No problems—I'm cleared. So is Kale.

Why am I surprised when Evan sets off the alarm?

Though he's dropped his phone, change, keys, watch, and pin into the bowl, he's evidently forgotten something in his shirt pocket. Once they wand him and pat him down, it turns out to be a stainless steel pen. They examine it and give it back to him.

After we clear security, we get our visitors' badges.

At last we head for the elevators, Evan preoccupied with his phone now that he's got it back.

I exhale quietly in relief. We're through security! We're in. Now we can focus on finding my mom.

The elevator doors slide closed behind us, and we all look at each other nervously. "Ready?" I ask.

Kale nods.

"Sure thing." Lacey licks her lips.

Evan inclines his head, but shifts his weight from foot to foot. He swallows and loosens his tie.

And Luke . . . Luke says softly, "Good luck, Kari." Then he does the unbelievable. He steps forward and kisses me—on the cheek. In spite of my current appearance.

My heart rolls over while Lacey makes a rude retching noise from her corner of the elevator. And in case nobody hears that, she says, "Gaaaaag. *Seriously?*"

Luke Carson just kissed me! I can feel the blush suffusing my face, and my pulse hammers wildly. I think I might spontaneously combust.

"How sweet," Evan says. "How brotherly."

Luke flushes and shoots him a glance, but doesn't say anything.

Brotherly? Funny how one word can make all the

pleasure rush out of your body. I am left feeling exactly like waterlogged sand: flat, heavy, bereft of energy.

I hate Evan Kincaid.

But he's probably right. Luke kissed me on the cheek, not the lips. He didn't mean anything by it except friendship. I remind myself that we're not here for me to fulfill my fantasies with the boy of my dreams. We're here because my mom is caught in a nightmare and my dad is MIA.

The elevator doors open on Mr. Carson's floor seconds later.

"Testing: one, two, three." We hear Rita's voice in our earbuds.

"Copy," I say in a low voice. Everyone else does too.

"Okay, good. You guys can hear us. We *finally* patched into the network. So we have the security cameras in your area taken care of. They're frozen on images of empty hallways. There's only one issue: If you go more than three or four floors below ground level, we may not be able to help you. Kari, you can use either the laser devices with the golf sights or the small jammers I gave you on individual cameras. Those will disrupt the signals, but they'll also alert someone that the cameras aren't functioning properly. They'll send someone to check on them."

"Okay. Thanks, guys."

"Good luck."

Luke, whose face is still a little pink, heads for his father's office, just in case his dad does show up, or someone asks questions. The rest of us head for the maintenance stairs, but I almost have a stroke when we find that the door to them is locked.

"Crap!" I whisper.

"What's the problem?" Lacey asks, and steps in front of me. She slides a badge into the slot under the handle and pulls the door open. "*Après vous*," she says.

"Where did you get that?" I ask.

Evan chuckles. "I'll wager it belongs to Jake. Doesn't it, Lacey? You palmed it when you kissed him, you shameless little hussy."

She smirks but doesn't deny it.

I stare at her with unwilling admiration. "Lacey, you have the makings of a world-class criminal."

She flashes her pearly whites at me. "Thanks."

We start descending flights of stairs, Evan checking out Lacey's legs as we go.

At each landing we come to we open the door and check around, but don't have much luck. Floors one and two are composed of long corridors: nothing but taupe tiles and office after office.

"I thought you knew where the detention center was?" Kale asks Lacey.

She grimaces. "Yeah . . . it's just that everything looks the same, and I can't remember exactly which floor it was on. I was kind of upset the day I was here."

On the third floor down there's a young analyst working in an office by himself. He looks up from his desk, focuses on us, and frowns. "Can I help you?" He rises and walks toward us.

We flash our visitors' passes. "School tour group," Evan calls.

"Where's your guide?"

"Uh . . ." I scramble for an answer as my pulse kicks into overdrive.

He shakes his head and picks up his phone. "We don't give public tours, especially for this building. I'm calling security."

Lacey steps forward. "Hi, I'm Lacey Carson. My dad's the director of the Agency. We have a specially arranged tour." She unclips her ID pass and hands it to him.

"Oh," he says, uncertainly, looking from it to her boobs, which she's thrust forward. He catches himself and checks the ID again.

She gives him a dazzling smile, and he blinks at its radiance. "But thanks for being cautious. I mean, we could be plaid-clad terrorists, bent on world destruction, right?" She laughs—with just the right amount of mockery and friendliness combined—and tosses that all-American blond hair of hers.

He's forced to laugh too, or look like an idiot.

She's masterful at peer pressure, even on a man twice her age.

He folds like a cheap lawn chair. "Well, enjoy your visit. Is there anything I can show you?"

"Nah, but thanks. We're meeting Dad in a couple of minutes. Just looking for a restroom?"

"Go back the way you came and up to the ground floor. They'll be on the left as you come out of the elevators."

Mr. Junior Analyst (or whatever he is) goes back to his desk and we scram.

The fourth floor down yields only empty offices. On the fifth floor we encounter a janitor in a steel blue uniform with the name AL stitched on his breast pocket. Unlike the analyst, Al isn't buying our story, no matter how jiggly and giggly Lacey gets.

Al glowers at us from under bushy gray eyebrows and growls, "I don't care who your daddy is." He points behind him. "You'll come into this office right here and wait while I call upstairs."

Kale and I exchange a glance.

"Okay, sir, whatever you say." We follow him into the deserted office, and I pull the door shut behind us. It clicks shut quietly as Al picks up a phone on the corner of the desk. As he presses the on button, Kale loops one arm around Al's neck in a choke hold.

"Christ! What are you doing?" Evan exclaims.

I gesture at him to shut up.

It takes less than a minute to drop the poor old guy to the floor.

"Sorry, Al," I say as we gently haul him a couple of doors down to a supply closet, and Lacey locks him in with his own keys.

"That was assault," Evan points out. "Or battery. Or both."

"You have a problem with those?" I ask serenely.

His mouth drops open. When he shuts it again, there's an odd little smile playing around his lips. "I'm developing a whole new level of respect for you, Kari Andrews."

"Louise," I correct him.

"Right."

"And it's about time," I add.

"Darling," he says. "I'll be damned if I'm not falling in love with you . . . especially since your hot new makeover."

Lacey snorts.

I shoot the finger at him. "Can we get on with finding my mom, now?"

Chapter Thirteen

We've descended seven flights of stairs when we finally reach a level of the building that isn't labeled. There's no number and no letter designating it, even to maintenance people. Interesting. And telling. This must be the floor where they've got my mother, surely? The nonexistent "detainee" floor?

"Lacey?" I ask, turning to her. "Is this it?"

She's looking into a compact mirror and applying lip gloss as we walk. "Huh?" She lifts her eyes and glances around. "Oh. Yeah. We've found it."

No thanks to her. I reach for the door handle.

"Wait!" she hisses. "There are guards on the other side."

Crap. "How many?"

"Two."

"Armed?"

"Yup. Some kind of handguns. In holsters at the waist."

"Bloody hell," Evan says.

Kale shrugs. "We'll have to take them out."

"Are you all mad?" Evan throws up his hands.

"I'll distract them." Lacey unbuttons her shirt another three inches. She's wearing a silver lace push-up bra, and it reveals her twin, uh, snowy mountains. I think a helicopter could go down between them and never be seen again.

Evan is stunned into appreciative silence.

Kale too.

"Kale," I order, "you take the left guard. I'll take the right." Despite my calm tone, my body buzzes with anticipatory adrenaline. My palms flood with sweat, and I have to focus on keeping my knees loose and my lower back relaxed.

Meanwhile, the guys are goggling like idiots at Lacey's boobs.

"Kale!"

"Huh?"

Disgusted, I repeat myself.

Kale nods.

I take a deep breath. "Let's go."

Lacey snicks Jake's card through the slot and pulls open the door. "Hi!" she exclaims. The guards are sitting in plastic chairs on opposite sides of the hallway.

Kale's guard drops the newspaper he's reading and just about swallows his tongue.

My guard smiles at Lacey. "You again?"

"Michael," Lacey coos.

Then everything's a blur as I lunge forward and plant my foot on his jaw, knocking him clean off the chair and onto the floor. His head cracks against the tiles, disorienting him, but he has the presence of mind to grab for the gun in his holster.

I stomp on his wrist with the full force of my hundred-odd pounds, and it snaps like a chicken bone. He gets out half a scream before I smother it with my hand and shove the barrel of his own gun smack in the middle of his forehead.

Meanwhile, Kale is the very soul of efficiency. He's simply tossed his guard's gun down the hallway and pinned the guy to the wall by the neck. He's choked him out cold. Kale is talented that way.

He raises his eyebrows at me, as if to imply that I'm slow.

"Naptime, buddy." I smash the butt of the gun into my guard's skull and knock him into unconsciousness.

I stand up and wipe my palms on my skirt as Lacey looks down at him regretfully, her shiny lip gloss glinting under the fluorescent lighting.

"Poor Michael," she says. "He gives a *great* back massage." She shivers with remembered pleasure.

"He'll live. And he'll still be hot with a goose egg," I tell her. I frown at him, though. Was this a bit too easy? And we've had no time to try to disable the security cameras. But that can't be helped now.

Evan shakes his head.

We move cautiously down the hallway, looking to the right and left. Weird: There isn't a single office—and stranger still, not even a room that connects with the corridor. It's a hallway to nowhere.

"All right," I say. "We're going to need to split up into two teams."

Lacey glances from Evan to Kale to me. "I'll go with Evan," she says, automatically picking the best-looking guy with the most money.

I shake my head. "No, actually you won't."

The princess is displeased. "Excuse me? Who are you to give me orders?"

Under Evan's amused gaze, I explain to her. "Neither you nor Evan is a trained fighter. What happens if you run into trouble? So you, Lacey, are going to go with Kale—unless you'd rather go with me?"

She pouts. But in the end it's an easy choice for her. After all, she doesn't like me much, and then there's the fact that Kale is a guy. Lacey will always take the opportunity to flirt with the opposite sex.

"Oh, *fine*," she says. "Whatever."

Thanks, mouths Kale to me behind her back.

Evan puts a hand over his heart in mock relief, looks down at me from his superior height, and murmurs, "I'm *so* relieved that I have you to protect me."

"Laugh all you want," I retort. "You'll be glad when the time comes."

"I'm sure."

Rita's voice suddenly chirps in my earbud. "Hey, kids." She sounds like she's inside a tin can.

"Hey. How're you doing?"

"Well, we lost you for a few, but we've now managed to tap into the security cameras on this level after all, so we can see your adorable faces."

A corner of Evan's mouth quirks. As if he had anything to do with it. I've given up trying to understand the guy.

"Great," I say. "Helps to have geniuses for friends and relatives."

"But I can't mess with the feed. Anything I do will just generate static and get you guys discovered. So keep your jammer and the laser device handy, okay?"

"Not a problem," I tell her. "So what else can you see?"

"Just a long corridor with no apparent doors. Weird."

"Yeah. Okay, well, keep in touch."

Evan and I keep going down our end of the hallway. How is it possible that it's just a lighted tunnel with no doors? There has to be a door to *something*. This makes no sense.

I can smell Evan's cologne as we walk along, as well as the starch of his shirt and his designer deodorant. What does it say about a guy that even his deodorant smells like it was custom-made? I mean, who does he think he is, the president?

In contrast, Luke smells like a normal guy—clean and sporty and sexy in a very approachable way. I think of his kiss . . . and then get mad at myself. This is *so* not the time.

The corridor takes a sharp turn to the right, so we do too. And fifteen feet down it's a dead end. I can't help a little noise of disappointment.

Evan's expression is puzzled, but thoughtful. "Huh."

"What do we do? Turn around? This is nuts," I say.

Rita's voice echoes in our ears. "Evan and Kari, look sharp. There are two people headed your way."

"Male? Female? What?" Evan asks.

"Can't tell. The angle is bad and so is the lighting."

Great. I open my mouth to say it, but am suddenly spun by the shoulders and slammed up against the wall. Mr. Pretentious Pits, Man of the Designer Deodorant, growls, "You sexy little troll." He covers my mouth with his obnoxious one—and the next thing I know, he's kissing me.

Kissing. Me.

Evan.

"Woo woo!" Rita says into my Kennedy Prep pin/comm unit.

He tastes of cinnamon. . . .

And his mouth is gentle, but firm. You could almost say insistent.

If this were anyone other than Evan Kincaid, International Jerk of Mystery, Mr. Brass Bollocks himself, it might not be a completely unpleasant experience.

But it is him.

And now he is trying to suck on my tongue.

I put a stop to that and bite his just as I hear Charlie's snicker through my comm unit.

Then I crouch low and spring up high, bringing my arms out so that I break Evan's hold on me and knock his arms aside. I clock him in the temple with a fist, and while he's still reeling from that, I turn and drive my elbow into his gut.

"Holy shit!" Rita says.

I spin, poised like a boxer, ready for the intruders, and Evan is doubled over, wheezing and gasping, when I realize that Kale and Lacey have witnessed everything. *They* are the intruders.

Lacey's mouth hangs open.

Kale shakes his head. "Mighty Mouse," he says to me. "No mercy?"

I barely restrain a snarl. I cannot even verbalize how pissed off I am.

He goes to Evan and puts a hand on his shoulder. "You okay, man?"

Evan manages only a heartfelt "Shite!" and gingerly touches his tongue. Where are his snide little comments now?

"Apologize, or I will take you down and stomp on your kidneys," I threaten.

Lacey's eyes, already round, widen to the size of dinner plates.

"I thought they were security guards," Evan says, but since he's got his tongue between his fingers, it comes out as "I thaw they wuh thecurity gods." He shrugs and wipes his hand on his pants. "Anyway, it always works in the American movies!"

"*Moron*," I say. I am even more furious that everyone *saw* him kiss me.

"Mighty Mouse?" Evan queries Kale.

"It's an old cartoon. Mouse as Superman. My dad showed it to me."

Evan turns to me.

I squint at him. "Do. Not. Call. Me. That."

"Super Shrew then." He says it decisively.

Kale laughs. "Don't try to tame her."

"Shut up! Both of you." I turn to Lacey. "What have you guys found on this floor?"

"A big load of nothing." She's still eyeing me warily.

I sigh. "Same here." I think for a moment. "There has to be a hidden door or panel somewhere."

Kale nods. "There's no way that the Agency would waste space on a secret, roomless corridor to nowhere."

We all start running our hands up and down the plain white walls. "Rita?" I speak into my comm unit/pin. "Can you guys see anything?"

"Negative," she says.

"Charlie?" I ask.

"No."

I'm duckwalking down the hallway now, feeling along the lower two feet of wall.

"Hey, Super Shrew," Evan calls.

I ignore him.

"Hallo?" He's not taking the hint.

A few moments of silence pass when nobody says anything, but I can hear everyone's palms whispering along the walls as we look for any sign of a hidden door.

Then I can feel someone come up behind me. It better not be Evan. . . .

Kale's voice says, "Man, I really wouldn't do that—"

And I feel a pinch on my behind.

I shoot upright, whirl, and kick out with my heel, catching Evan squarely in the chest. He flies backward. The look of shock on his face is priceless. He hits the wall with his shoulders, then his head.

"Bloody *hell*," he says, and slides down the wall. He sprawls there, dazed.

But I barely hear him.

Evan's thick head has hit the button we're looking

for. A panel slides open right above him, and inside the panel is a keypad. Below the keypad is a slot for a security badge.

"Lacey?" I gesture toward it.

She steps forward, her knee bumping Evan's shoulder, and slides the badge she stole from Jake through the slot.

A hidden door opens.

Evan is so out of it that he doesn't even think to look up her skirt.

Chapter Fourteen

"Awesome," Rita says into our comm units.

"You found it!" Charlie screams in my ear.

"Yeah, kiddo, we did."

"When all else fails," he says solemnly, "resort to violence."

Evan heaves himself to his feet. "What would you do without me?" he asks, and with a sweep of his hand, invites us to go into the newly revealed space.

I look nervously at the security camera. It occurs to me again that this has all been a little too easy—but I shrug off the idea. I want to find my mom.

We all exchange glances and step through the door.

It's a little disconcerting that it immediately slides closed behind us. But I remind myself that we do still have Jake's key—and if it worked on the outside, then surely it will work on the inside.

The other thing I notice is that I no longer hear Charlie's breathing in my ear. "Kiddo?"

No response.

"Rita?"

Nothing.

"Can anyone hear Rita or Charlie?" I ask.

Everyone tries to talk to them, but nobody makes contact. Our comm units have gone dead. Wonderful.

I look around. It's dark in here, and the walls are ugly, rough concrete with no decorative touches whatsoever. We move down a poorly lit hallway to another door, which is locked. I cut my eyes toward Lacey, and she works her magic again with Jake's badge.

The door opens.

And there, staring at us, is another guard.

Kale and I exchange one glance and launch forward in tandem before the man can even think about drawing his weapon. He's so stunned at the sight of two prep-school kids flying toward him that he doesn't know how to react—and this is what we're counting on.

I slam the full force of my 110 pounds into his right knee. He howls.

At the same time Kale smashes his own forehead into the man's, claps his hands over the guy's ears, hard, and then drives his fists into each temple. The guard drops like a stone.

Lacey steps forward and relieves him of his badge. She swipes the badge through the slot on the door, and presto! We move into a T-intersection that marks a hidden world. We've made it to Langley's secret detention center.

On either side of us are heavily reinforced steel doors, scarred with use. Each door has a small metal flap at the top so that you can peer inside, and a narrow slot at the bottom that's probably for sliding in trays of bad industrial food.

My heart sinks at the thought that my mom may be trapped behind one of these depressing doors. This place is awful.

It's also deserted, which seems strange. My nose starts to itch, but I ignore it. We're so close to finding my mother . . . we have to be.

"Okay," I say. "Lacey and Kale, you go to the right. Evan and I will go to the left"—I swing toward him with a glare—"and if you try anything again, if you lay a finger on me, I will yank off your balls and use them as hacky sacks. Got it?"

He nods. To his credit he doesn't even smirk. But as I set off down our section of the hallway, he says, "So bloodthirsty . . . I find that devastatingly attractive in a girl."

I turn and squint at him with menace.

Evan holds up his hands, palms toward me, in a gesture of surrender. I note with satisfaction that he still has my dusty footprint on his shirt.

He notices what I'm fixated on and reads my smug little smile like a book. "I'll never wash this shirt again," he says.

Right. This from the guy who was just ogling Lacey's assets.

I peer into the first cell through the little eye-level

flap. Nobody inside. "The last thing I need right now is your crap, Evan! I'm worried sick about my mother." I move to the next cell. Nobody in there, either.

"I know," he says quietly. "Maybe I was trying to take your mind off that."

I turn my head and stare at him. He's absolutely serious. And his gray eyes hold compassion. I don't know how to deal with this. So I just keep searching cells. Nothing in number three. Or number four. I open the little flap on number five, and almost turn away with a sigh.

But a dark lump in the corner catches my eye.

I look again . . . it's a human figure, female, curled in a fetal position on the single bed. "Mom?"

The figure bolts upright and stares. Then she springs off the bed and lunges for the door. "Kari? Oh, my God, *Kari*?" Somehow she can tell it's me, even through the troll makeup and hair.

"Mom!" I yank on the door handle, but it won't budge. My first instinct is to kick down the damned door, but it's at least six inches thick and made of steel. I'll break my foot on the first attempt.

Evan hears me and comes running. He shouts for Kale and Lacey while I question my mom. She looks terrible . . . pale and exhausted, her normally chic dark hair disheveled. She's barefoot.

"Why are you here?" I demand, as she asks simultaneously, "How did you find me?" She takes in my appearance. "Nice disguise."

"Are you okay? What is going on?" I blurt, while she asks, "Where's Charlie? Is he all right?"

141 / TWO LIES AND A SPY

"Charlie's fine," I say.

"Your father and I are accused of being double agents."

"*What? Why?* And where's Dad?"

"I don't know where your father is." There are fine lines of strain around her eyes, and she's got dark circles underneath them. She's clearly not had a shower and has slept in her clothes. Her makeup is smeared, but she still looks beautiful. And my heart aches for her.

"Kari," Mom says. "I don't know how you got in here, but I guarantee that you wouldn't be inside unless the Agency wanted you to be. This is a trap—you need to get out of here while you still can."

I ignore this. "Why would the Agency think you guys have been turned? That is *ridiculous!*"

"I don't know why they'd suspect it."

Kale and Lacey have come running.

"Lacey, the badge?" I prompt. "We've got to get my mom out of here. This is crazy."

Lacey snicks the badge through the slot on the door, and I yank on the handle. Nothing happens. "Try again?"

She does.

I still can't get the door open. I pound on it with my fist in frustration. "Do you still have the other badge?"

Lacey nods.

"Try that."

She does. No dice.

Unbelievable.

"Kari," Mom says urgently. "This is a trap. You have to get yourself out of here. Don't worry about me."

"I'm not leaving without you!" I can't believe she's even suggesting this.

"You'll have to. Go. Get out of here!"

"There has to be a way through this door," I insist. I turn to Kale. "What if we both kicked at the same time? Do you think we could dislodge the door from the hinges?"

Kale looks it up and down, then slowly shakes his head.

I pound on it again, in frustration. *Think, Kari.*

But I don't have the chance. My mom is right: We've walked into a trap.

I hear quick, heavy footsteps coming from both directions. Before I can even react, we're surrounded by agents.

Not just any old agents. My good buddy Mitch heads them up. I'm happy to see that in addition to his broken nose and swollen eyes, he now has a nasty red weal around his neck.

He gives me a death stare. "Thanks for visiting, Karina."

"Have you missed me?" I ask.

"Yeah. Quite a bit. Tell me, Miss Smarty-Pants, didn't it seem just a little too easy for you to 'break in' to Langley? Or are you so impressed with yourself that you never questioned that?"

I glare right back at him. "Oh, so five Agency employees are just *faking* unconsciousness? What about you, the other day? Did you have to call for help to untangle yourself from my little brother's backpack?"

Mitch turns almost purple with rage. "Shut up and come quietly. As you can see, you kids are outnumbered."

I put my hands on my hips. "I'll come with you once you release my mother."

Mitch gives a short bark of laughter. "I'll release your mother when hell freezes over, young lady. The bitch is a traitor and a moneygrubbing wh—"

I lunge at Mitch. *Nobody* calls my mom a traitor and gets away with it. But this time he's more prepared for me. He simply steps aside, and my heel smashes into the gut of the agent behind him. The guy goes down clutching his stomach. I jump over him and slam my head and elbow into the next man, sending him reeling against the wall. But he recovers and comes for me.

My mom screams at me from her cell. "Kari! What are you doing?"

I pull Lacey's cumbersome pillow out of my waistband and toss it aside as Evan and Kale jump into the fray. Kale takes down a blond agent with a blow to the side of his neck, while Evan tackles the one who's trying to corral me, jumping on his back and getting him in a choke hold.

Kale goes for a female agent next, but she puts up a good fight.

The guy under Evan spins and drives back deliberately into the wall, slamming Evan against it. But somehow Evan recovers, slips off him, and smashes the man's skull into it in return.

I have a split second to wonder if Evan has had some training after all? But then why was he so unprepared for me?

I don't have time to wonder long.

Lacey, who's been standing on the sidelines until now, suddenly vaults into the fray, jumping on the back of yet another agent and taking him by surprise. Typical Lacey, though: Her little plaid skirt flies up and exposes her underwear as she rides the man like a bronco. Her panties are pink. And tiny.

I launch myself again at Mitch. I am bent on pulverizing the rest of his face. I'm going to break his jaw. I'm going to rip off his lips. I'm going to—

Someone in the background yells, "Hey! What in the hell is going on here?"

I see Luke out of the corner of my eye.

Luke? What is he . . . ?

Someone grabs me out of the air, by the waist. I am yanked backward. I kick and flail but don't manage to make contact with my latest attacker. "Let me go!" I yell.

"Easy, Shrew," Evan's voice says, as he carries me several feet away from Mitch. "It's over."

I spend an undignified moment dangling from his arm. It's true—everyone has stopped fighting. Why?

Because Mr. Carson, Director of the Agency, is standing in front of us looking like blue thunder. And lined up with him are Luke, Rita, and Charlie.

"Charlie! Are you okay?"

"Yup." He pushes up his horn-rims as he looks pointedly at Evan.

Evan sets me on my feet, and Charlie gives him a thumbs-up.

"Rita?" I query. "Luke? You two okay?"

They nod. The expressions on their faces reflect what I

already know: that we are in deep, deep trouble. Titanic-level trouble.

"Young lady," grates out Mr. Carson. "I need your word and the word of your friends that you will come quietly now, without any further nonsense."

"Karina, do what he says," Mom calls from her cell.

I gulp in some air and look sideways at Kale. My mom is still a prisoner, and I'm not at all sure that I want to give up and leave her here.

Kale raises an eyebrow, asking me what I want to do.

I wipe some sweat away from my temples and turn to Mr. Carson again. "And I'd like your word that you'll release my mother. The charges against her are crazy, and you must know that."

"We are investigating the charges," he says neutrally. "That's all I can tell you at this time."

"But they'll be dropped," I say. "That's what I can tell *you* at this time. My parents are not traitors." I'm furious.

Mr. Carson's mouth tightens. "Let's go, people."

I'm hustled towards the door. "Mom!" I yell. "I will get you out of here." She makes no reply.

We are escorted out of the "non-existent" detention facility and hustled back into the corridor to nowhere. We take the elevator to a different floor and walk down several more utilitarian hallways.

Finally we arrive at a door that only Mr. Carson has access to. He swipes his badge through the slot, and we're taken into yet another high-security area with central reception and eight rooms radiating off it.

Mr. Carson directs the agents to separate each of us into our own room.

"I don't think so," I say.

He raises his eyebrows at me.

"My brother Charlie is only seven years old. I won't have him traumatized and interrogated like a criminal. He stays with me."

Mr. Carson opens his mouth, probably to inform me that I'm not the one giving orders, but Luke intercedes.

"Dad," he says. "Please. The kid is terrified."

Adaptable as always, Charlie gazes up at Mr. C. with huge owl eyes behind his horn-rims, and his mouth trembles just the right amount. Good boy.

"Fine," Mr. Carson says. "Luke, I'll deal with you later." Then he turns on his heel and walks off.

Luke looks dejected, and I feel terrible.

I don't know how to salvage things with the boy of my dreams. Note to self: The way to a guy's heart is *not* to manipulate him into betraying his father.

"Luke, I'm so sorry for getting you into this," I say.

"It's okay." He runs a hand through his hair. "Given your circumstances, I'd have done the same thing."

"Really?" My silly heart beats with hope.

He meets my gaze for a long moment, then swallows and sets his jaw. A tiny muscle jumps at the side of it. "Yeah. Really."

I want to throw my arms around his neck and shout, *I love you!*

But I don't.

I am led away with Charlie and shoved into a room to

await whatever fate has in store for us. The door is locked with finality.

Five minutes later, though, it opens again and Evan Kincaid is shoved inside with us.

Ugh.

Chapter Fifteen

The room that we find ourselves in is a study in gray and blue. The floor is gray industrial tile with tiny flecks of black and cream in it. I have lots of time to examine it while my feet are planted, one each, in a twelve-inch square—as if I'm about to sink into cement blocks.

The walls are gray too, like the overcast sky outside. Gloomy, cold gray like my mood, and like Evan's eyes at the moment. I have to admit that I'm glad of his company, because I know that I'm in over my head.

The furniture looks like it was all turned off the same assembly line at the same factory in the same hour: cheap, blond wood frames and navy upholstery that people's butts and backs have worn nubby. The armrests are dark and stained with use.

Charlie curls up on a sofa, his feet tucked underneath him.

Evan sits casually on the arm of a matching chair and folds his arms across his chest.

I sit somberly next to Charlie and stare into space, a million thoughts chasing each other through my head. What will happen to Mom? Where is Dad? What kind of trouble are we in? Will my friends' parents kill them, and then me for getting them into this?

Will we be thrown into a jail for kids? Will we be prosecuted? Hacking. False IDs. Breaking and entering. Assaulting agents. We're in deep.

"So," Evan says.

It occurs to me that I should be grateful to him. How weird. "Thanks for your help back there," I say. "For once, you weren't completely useless."

His mouth turns up at one corner. "You're welcome."

I rerun my splintered mental images of him during the fight with the agents and frown. "You actually seemed to know what you were doing."

"Beginner's luck," he tells me, but it sounds like a rote answer.

I narrow my eyes on him. "Must be. Right? Because otherwise I wouldn't have been able to disable you so quickly, *twice*."

He sighs, steeples his fingers under his chin, and peers at me over them. "Kari," he says. "I'm not even sure how to tell you this. . . ."

What could Evan Kincaid, International Jerk of Mystery, have to tell me?

Eww. I seriously cannot believe that he kissed me. Worse, that it was my very first real kiss by any boy on the planet.

I was saving that for Luke Carson, if I ever got the chance.

"Let me guess," I say to Evan. "I got you pregnant when you kissed me?"

Charlie falls into a fit of the giggles.

"Yes," says Evan. "That's exactly it. I'm pregnant and alone. What will I do?"

Charlie stops laughing. "Wait," he says. "Boys can't get pregnant, can they?"

Now it's Evan's turn to laugh, and mine.

"No," he says.

"Nobody can get pregnant from a kiss," I tell Charlie. It's too funny that he has memorized half of *Roget's Thesaurus* and knows how electricity works and can write computer code, but he is truly lost when it comes to the basics of life.

"Just humiliated, disgusted, and slimed," I add, turning to glare at Evan.

"*Slimed?*" He looks offended.

"Yes. Like the trail a snail leaves, when it crawls up a window?"

"I know what it means," Evan growls.

"Oh, good." I aim a sunny smile in his direction. "I didn't know what you Brits called it, what with the term 'snogging' and all that. So I figured I should translate."

"Shrew," he mutters.

"Wait," says Charlie. "So are you saying that you don't like Evan that way?"

"What way?"

"*That* way," my brother says. "*You* know."

"No, of course I don't like Evan that way!"

If possible, Evan looks even more offended. "Well," he

says to nobody in particular. "Who needed an ego, anyhow? Useless buggers, really. I'll just discard mine now, since it will never recover."

"Are you done talking to yourself?" I ask him.

"Not quite. I was just getting to the reassurance and the positive self-affirmations, actually."

"Well, when you're done with those, you can tell me whatever it is that you don't know how to tell me."

He expels a breath and gazes at me sardonically. "Thank you."

"No problem." I wait, the picture of polite expectation.

"Kari, I'm . . . not who you think I am."

I raise my eyebrows. "No?"

He shakes his head.

"You mean you're really a nice guy without a shred of pretension who's never been a serial flirt?"

"Wow," he says, clearly stung. "You don't pull your punches, do you?"

"Never."

"All right. Then I won't bother to be sensitive or delicate about this. I'm not just a high school kid, Kari. I'm an Interpol agent. Well, agent-in-training."

I gape at him.

Then I snort.

And finally, since his expression doesn't change, I burst out laughing. "Of course you are, Evan."

"Kincaid," Charlie says in a fake British accent. He lowers his glasses and peers over them. "Evan Kincaid. Double-oh seven."

Evan sighs. "You two done snickering yet?"

"No. At least I'm not. Charlie?"

My little brother thinks about it. "Yeah, I guess so."

"Tell us another one, Evan," I challenge.

"I'm not joking. I'm in training as an Interpol agent."

"And M gave you your diploma, right?" I'm so not swallowing this huge lie.

Evan stands up and pulls his wallet from his pocket. He opens it and fishes out an ID that says he, E. Kincaid, is a junior agent with Interpol.

I give it back to him. "I can buy a shiny plastic sheriff's badge in Walmart."

He nods, then pokes his tongue into his cheek. "Call the number on my ID. See who answers."

"Good bluff, since they took our cell phones."

"For the last bloody time, Kari, I'm not lying to you. I'm with Interpol."

I stare at him, look right into his eyes, and he's never been more serious. Unless he's the best con man in the western hemisphere, Evan is telling me the truth. They say the truth will set you free, right?

But it will also make you angry beyond belief. "If—*if* you are with Interpol, then what are you doing attending Kennedy Prep in Washington, DC?" I demand.

"What better place to put me during training?" Evan asks. "I become known and loved—"

I snort again.

"—by the sons and daughters of America's power elite. I keep my ear to the ground and report on any suspicious goings-on, and I train with the best agents and weapons experts in the business."

I look down at my hands, which are clasped fiercely

in my lap so that they won't shake with rage. The tips of my fingers are white with the pressure. " You've been spying on all of us. Slithering around like the snake that you are."

He sighs. "I knew you would take this brilliantly."

"Do you not have a conscience? Don't you feel the least bit ashamed of yourself?" My voice is rising, but I can't help it.

"Kari, you don't understand—"

"I understand perfectly!" I flash. "There's nothing wrong with my powers of deductive reasoning! You are scum, Kincaid. I should have driven a Kennedy Prep pen through your carotid artery the first time I met you—"

Charlie winces and I force myself to shut up.

Evan shakes his head. His eyes have gone blue again. I should have known not to trust a guy whose eyes don't even stay the same color from moment to moment.

"God, you're beautiful when you're angry," he says. "Even under that hideous troll makeup."

I grind my teeth together. "You just can't stop, can you?"

He looks at me quizzically. "Stop what?"

"Manipulating and flirting and . . . and . . . being snaky."

"Snaky," he says thoughtfully. "I don't think that's a word."

"Yes, it is!" Charlie informs him. "You can find it in *Roget's* under 'cunning.'"

"Ah. Well. I stand corrected," Evan concedes.

"Actually, you're sitting," Charlie points out.

"True. You're very observant, Charlie-my-man."

I'm ready to bang my head against the wall.

"Kari," Evan says. "I'm sorry. It's not as if I set out to deceive you—"

"Yes, you did." I get up and stalk to the other side of the room. "Just don't talk to me right now. I have nothing—less than nothing—to say to you. I only want to get out of this place and find my dad and free my mom, and never see you again."

I kick the wall. "How long is it going to take to get some answers and get out of here?"

As if someone is listening, the handle on the door depresses. Then the door opens, and Mr. Carson walks in with an old-fashioned accordion file. "Evan. Charlie. You're excused for the moment. Agent Smith, outside, will take you to another office."

"Charlie stays with me," I say.

"Charlie," emphasizes Mr. Carson, "will be just fine. He will not be interrogated without you present. All right? I need to speak with you alone, Karina."

I give Evan a long, menacing stare. "You owe it to me to make sure he's okay."

"Hell-o," Charlie announces. "I'm right here, people. Will you stop talking *about* me and talk *to* me, instead?"

"Sorry, kiddo," I say. "I just want to make sure you're all right."

"I'm fine. And I want to ask Evan questions about Interpol. So stop worrying." Charlie walks over to the loathsome Brit and slips his hand into his, which makes me want to throw up. Evan himself seems a little taken aback, but he looks down at Charlie with a smile that can almost be described as sweet.

"Karina?" says Mr. Carson.

"Yes?" I turn and stare into his eyes, so like Luke's and yet harder, more tired, and older.

"Have a seat," he orders.

I do. So does he. And then the door closes behind Evan and Charlie, leaving me completely alone with the director of the Agency.

Chapter Sixteen

The atmosphere in the room is thick with my own attitude and resentment and fear. It's just as thick with
something weighty Mr. Carson has to tell me and his
annoyance that a bunch of prep-school kids have made a
mockery of Langley's agents and its security guards, and
done it with his own son's help.

I guess I can't blame the man for being pissy.

But I'm feeling the same way because of this royal
screwup with my mom.

Mr. Carson pulls over a table so that it's positioned
between us. He takes the elastic band off the accordion
file and sets it in his lap. Then he removes a bunch of
white papers and places them on the table for me.

I scan the headings, which scream things like AGENCY
INFILTRATED BY RUSSIAN SPIES.

How dramatic and deluded.

I know my parents. My mother is a person of total integrity, and she would never do this. I know my dad, too. He wouldn't be a party to any of it—ever. Neither of them would expose their children to the dangers of becoming double agents either. They may be gone a lot, and that's hard, but they are gone for the right reasons.

I curl my lip as I read the paper on top of the stack.

TOP SECRET—EYES ONLY

SUBJECT: Agency employees Andrews, Irene and Andrews, Calvin

SUMMARY: Two veteran Agency employees have worked as double agents loyal to Russia for over twenty years.

BACKGROUNDS: Andrews, Irene (nee Irina) is of Russian extraction. Parents entered U.S. as poor refugees seeking political asylum from Communism. Irene Andrews first traveled to Russia on a study-abroad program in Moscow during her junior year at *Georgetown University. It is likely that she was first recruited for Russian intelligence work during that time.

Andrews, Calvin is American born, of Scots/English extraction. Parents also American born. He appears to have had no formal education after the high school level as he joined the army at age 18 and quickly distinguished himself as a sharp-shooter of great skill. Andrews was stationed at the U.S. Embassy in Moscow in 1989, where he met Irene and established friendships with Russians of dubious character.

ANALYSIS AND CONCLUSIONS: For the past decade the Agency has tracked the Andrews's movements, investigated their contacts, and gathered evidence, tracing a complex trail of payments for their services. The money originates with a former faction of the KGB and is laundered through several international banks and businesses until it finds a home with a shell corporation in the Caymans, owned by a mysterious conglomerate.

Since Irene Andrews has not only been an analyst for the past seven years but travels extensively to lead missions and head up field analytics, she is in the ideal position to pass information and sensitive documents through her husband, a field agent. They have taken full advantage of their positions and the couple has profited handsomely from them, as the internal sting operation has revealed.

I finish reading this preposterous document and stack it neatly on top of all the other ones. I push the pile back toward Mr. Carson and fold my hands on the table in front of me.

There are times when it's best to be Miss Manners, and then there are times when force and crudeness are the most effective approach. I choose the second option. "With all due respect, Mr. Carson, this is a load of crap!"

He keeps his own hands flat on the table. His nails are square and trimmed, but not manicured. His wedding band is plain gold, as nondescript as they come. It screams WASP, just as much as his haircut and dark suit and tie do. No gaudy stones or textures for Mr. C. He's as conventional and "by the book" as they come. "I can understand that you don't want to accept this, Karina. This isn't information that anyone wants to discover about his or her parents."

"No, see, what you're not *getting* here is that none of this is true. I have spent sixteen years around these people, and"—I break off to laugh, while his expression doesn't change at all—"and I have seen them at all hours of the day and night, eating, working, talking, showering, cooking, parenting, paying bills, and stressing about things just like every normal American does. What I have *never* seen them doing is spying for Russia, or any other country than the United States. Don't you think I'd know, Mr. Carson? I cannot tell you how completely ridiculous and unfounded and . . . and . . . just *bullshit* this all is! These accusations are the biggest load of garbage."

Mr. Carson says nothing. He opens his handy-dandy accordion file once again and starts pulling out more stuff.

Mr. C. drops a stack of phone records in front of me that detail calls from my mom's cell phone to a local number that then routes them to numbers in Russia.

"Big deal," I say. "She speaks Russian; she runs ops there. Of course she calls Russia!" Too late I realize that this information is more damning than helpful.

"Exactly. So why would she try to cover her tracks by routing these calls through a DC exchange?"

I can't answer that.

Luke's dad then drops a pile of transcriptions in front of me. These are texts of Mom's phone calls, with a bunch of names blacked out, and even I have to admit they're suspicious.

"Of course she runs double games," I tell Mr. C. "That's the only way she can catch the bad guys."

He raises his eyebrows and dumps a bunch of papers having to do with my dad's calls and phone conversations in front of me. These are followed by stacks of pictures: Mom and Dad, both together and individually, leaving different buildings, talking on pay phones and unmarked prepaid phones like the ones in our backpacks, and meeting people whom evidently they're not supposed to meet.

"Did you track them to the toilet, too?" I ask. "Did you think a double flush was *sinister?*" My sarcasm has no effect on Mr. Carson. "What about to the pharmacy or the grocery store? Do you think it's suspect that Mom buys Flintstones vitamins for Charlie? Is it a sign of treason that sometimes Dad uses coupons? Or that sometimes we buy two steaks and freeze one?"

Mr. Carson sighs. He pulls a last stack of papers from the accordion file, followed by a small object that fits in his fist.

The papers are bank records from a private brokerage

on Grand Cayman. My parents have made a number of deposits and transfers there.

And the object is a tube of lipstick that I swear I've seen before. It's pale pink.

"Not my color," I say, "but thanks."

He taps it on the table, then uncaps it.

"You? I really think you'd look better in a red or a coral," I tell him.

He sets the tubular cap on the table, and then twists the bottom counterclockwise twice. He yanks it off. Inside is a tiny recessed compartment. He hands me the bottom, and I examine it.

"What is it?" I give it back.

"That is a device that replicates microchips," Mr. Carson says. "And it was found in your mother's purse."

I stare at it, then shake my head. "My mom doesn't use that brand."

"No?"

"She uses a lip palette and a brush, not a tube."

"Is that a fact?" Mr. Carson starts to gather up all of his documentation.

Too late I realize that I've made yet another damning statement. If my mom doesn't use lipstick like that, then the unspoken question is, why did they find it in her purse?

"Look, there has to be a mistake," I insist. "Maybe Mom lost her palette and brush on her last trip and had to buy a tube in the airport."

"Karina. Don't be willfully naive. Your parents have somehow been passing copies of top secret information to the Russians during their missions. More accurately, they've been passing it to a faction of the KGB that never dissolved."

"Ridiculous!"

"So you're not helping them?"

I gape at Mr. Carson. "Me?"

"What about your brother?"

"*Charlie*? Are you *insane*? He's seven years old!"

Mr. Carson spreads his hands, palm up. "How is that relevant?"

I jump to my feet and push back from the table. I have listened while he's talked trash about my parents. I can even take him accusing me. But I will not tolerate this attack on an innocent kid. "We're done here," I inform him. "With all due respect, Mr. Carson, you must have gotten into a cache of LSD left over from Agency experiments in the sixties. Are you seriously asking me whether Charlie is a mustache-twirling, international villain?"

"Calm down, Kari."

"I won't!"

"Please. Sit down. These are questions that, unfortunately, I have to ask. And it's possible that you and Charlie have been used without your knowledge."

I shake my head. "No."

He gets up, rounds the table, and positions my chair again in front of it. He extends a hand in invitation for me to be seated.

To tell the truth, I'd rather kick his ass. But even as upset as I am, I know that's not a constructive way to proceed. So I sit down again.

Mr. Carson does too. He sighs. He reaches out and pats

my hand with sympathy. "Kari, I don't mean to upset you. I don't want to harass you. Perhaps you could think of this as an opportunity to help your parents and the Agency—to clear their names."

I narrow my eyes on him. "Don't try to snow me now."

"Let's entertain the crazy possibility that your parents are guilty, okay?" He holds up a hand at my expression. "Just bear with me for a moment, and let's say, hypothetically, that they are. Would you help them betray your country?"

"Of course not!"

"Even if they said their lives depended on it?"

"They'd never put me in that position."

"Never?"

I shake my head.

"What if they said Charlie's life depended on your cooperation with a foreign government?"

I open my mouth to say no, and then close it again.

Mr. Carson evaluates me silently. Then he nods. "We all have a weakness, Kari."

I fold my arms across my chest and avert my gaze.

"You're a good kid," Mr. C says, surprising me. "Your response just now tells me that you're no liar."

"Gee, thanks." My tone is heavy with sarcasm. "Can I have a lollipop now?"

He blows out an audible breath and gives me an odd, wry smile. "Imagine, the Director of the Agency, asking for help from a sixteen-year-old girl . . ."

I give him a sharp glance.

"Pretty far-fetched, isn't it?" He folds his hands on the

table. "But that's exactly what's happening here. We need your help, Karina. *I* need your help. Your country needs your help."

Funny, there's no indication from my BS detector nose that he's anything but sincere, whereas Mitch's lies had me sneezing within thirty seconds.

"Think carefully. Have you seen any odd scraps of information around your house or cars?"

"No."

"Lists of names, perhaps?"

"No," I say again.

"Have you witnessed anything in your parents' behavior that might indicate that they're transmitting data?"

"No! How many times do I have to say it?"

"Does anyone close to them do a lot of international travel?"

I think about it. "Sophie," I say reluctantly. "A family friend who's a photographer."

Mr. Carson clears his throat. "We've checked her out thoroughly. We've analyzed every image she's ever produced, uploaded, or e-mailed."

"Wow—how nice to know. Do you spy on her in the shower, too? Get some cheap thrills that way?" I know I'm being impossibly rude, but I feel violated on her behalf, as well as on my parents'.

He shakes his head. "I'm not the enemy, Kari. I don't deserve your anger. Neither do the Agency employees who've been assigned to this case."

The sound of my laughter is harsh and brittle, and it goes on far too long, even to my own ears. "Yeah," I say, after I pause for a breath. "That Mitch. He's a real peach."

Mr. Carson gives up on getting any useful information out of me and leaves. But my hopes of being released are dashed when two other agents come in and sit down across from me. They start to ask me questions that date back to when I was a toddler.

Do I remember my parents speaking Russian at home?

Of course I do. They met in Moscow, and they both speak it fluently.

Do I know of Russians who came to the house to socialize or do business?

Well, duh.

Who are these people?

I name a professor at Georgetown, a researcher at Dumbarton Oaks, a lawyer who deals with immigration issues. I also name a manicurist, a banker, and a tailor who services half of the Pentagon. These individuals are harmless and just make their living like everyone else. They're not spies or foreign agents, for God's sake.

Do I speak Russian?

I tell them I suck at languages. I can't even speak pig Latin.

They don't bother to ask about Charlie, and I don't offer the information.

They want to know if we eat traditional Russian dishes.

Really? Sure. My parents loaded my Similac with Smirnoff. I'm addicted to Borscht. I adore ice cream topped with caviar. Please!

They do not appreciate being mocked.

Well, I don't appreciate being interrogated.

We stare humorlessly at one another for a while, and then they begin with the questions again.

Do I dream in Russian?

I laugh hysterically at this. I have already told them I don't speak it, so why would I dream in it?

They ask me the value of the dollar to the ruble.

I have no clue.

What religion am I?

Officially? Baptist. But it's not like we really attend church.

How often do we go?

I don't know . . . a few times a year. Definitely Easter and Christmas.

What's our family's real religion?

Baptist. I spell it: b-a-p-t-i-s-t.

They don't appreciate the spelling part.

So we're not Russian Orthodox?

No.

Am I sure about that?

Yes.

Was I baptized Russian Orthodox?

Not to my knowledge, but I was only a few months old. I ask them if they recall their own baptisms, because if so, then they have incredible memories. I ask how they know that they weren't signed over to Satan at the age of three days?

I can tell that one of them wants to smack me. The other one moves around in his chair as if he has a really bad case of hemorrhoids but just gets on with the questioning.

Do I love my parents?

Duh.

Do I love them enough to lie for them?

Yes, but I'm not lying.

Do I love them enough to betray my country?

I tell them that I am beyond sick of their questions. I tell them that I want a glass of water.

They ignore me.

I repeat my request.

They ask me if I know the Pledge of Allegiance.

Yes.

Will I please recite it?

I do.

How do those words make me feel?

Huh? I don't know. Fine.

Proud to be an American?

Sure.

Or ashamed to be a traitor to my country, like my parents?

I tell them that they are brainwashed idiots, and that they are so far over the line.

What line would that be?

The line of common decency. The line of truth. The line where my parents and I are supposed to be considered innocent until proven guilty.

Am I quite sure that I'm not the one who's crossed the line? Me, and my parents, too? Is it decent to commit treason for money? Is it truthful to lie to them? And how can they consider us innocent when we are mired in hundreds of facts that point to our guilt?

I explode.

I tell them that if they ask me any more obnoxious questions, I will pulverize them.

They ask how long I've had these violent tendencies. And are they fantasies, or do I seriously consider acting on them?

Though I want to smash both of their faces in, I run to the door instead. I pound on it and scream that I am done, done, done with these assholes, and that someone had better let me out of here and give me access to an attorney, or I will contact our around-the-corner neighbor, who is a Supreme Court justice, and make them pay for this.

I demand to be assured of my brother's welfare.

I scream that they had better let my mother take a shower and give her clean clothes.

And I tell them that if anyone shoots my dad, I will make sure they are prosecuted to the fullest extent of the law.

The door opens while I am still pounding on it, and I fall forward. I'm so tired and frustrated that I've lost the ability to count on my reflexes. I trip and sprawl right into Evan Kincaid's arms.

And Charlie—seven-year-old Charlie—says to the agents behind me that they'd better stop harassing his sister, or they will have to answer to him.

I can't laugh, because there is a huge lump in my throat that my baby brother is doing his level best to be my pit bull and protector. And I can't sob, because I refuse to give any of these people the satisfaction of making me cry.

So I let Evan set me on my feet, and when he holds me away from him by the shoulders and asks me if I'm okay, I tell him that I've never been better.

Chapter Seventeen

It's after midnight when Agent A-hole and Agent
Hemorrhoid escort Evan, Charlie, and me to a concrete
box of a hotel. I don't even notice the name of it. They
have some sort of arrangement already with the desk,
because the receptionist hands them two plastic key
cards, and we proceed to the elevators, which are framed
by terrible fake ficus trees.

We are led to a room blander than grits—really, who
decorates these hotel rooms? Not that I care. The agents
seat themselves like two bookends at a square table near
the window, which has a gorgeous view of a dimly lit
parking garage.

"Get some rest," Agent A-hole orders.

I sprawl on one of the beds, even though there is no
way I'll sleep. Evan and Charlie sprawl on the other bed
together, which totally annoys me. Why isn't my brother

on my bed with me? Does he have to male-bond with *Evan*, of all people?

Only a couple of days ago I was wishing for a guy role model for Charlie. *Be careful what you wish for.*

"So," Evan says. "How are you doing, Kari?"

I turn my head and glare at him, then go back to staring into space. I have no desire to talk to him, the snake. Unbelievable that he's been masquerading among us as a regular teenager, spying and taking notes on everyone at Kennedy Prep. No, worse . . . he's probably been collecting damaging information about my parents! Why else would he force his company on me and Charlie?

"Ah." The jerk speaks again. "Very well, then. Glad I asked."

A half hour goes by in silence before Evan tries a second time. "You know, it's not as if I got you into this. *You* got *me* into this. So if anyone should be not speaking to someone, it should be me not speaking to you."

This, after he forced himself on us? I turn and evaluate him as if he is a cockroach. Then I look away again.

Charlie fidgets. "Can I have my laptop back?" he asks the agents.

"No," they both say simultaneously. Jerks.

"Then can I have a book?"

"Why don't you watch TV like a normal kid?" Agent Hemorrhoid recommends. "Reruns of *Dora the Explorer*, or *iCarly* or something." He tosses the remote control at Charlie, who misses it completely and looks over at me.

"My brother, who is seven, is better read than both of you apes," I tell them. "He doesn't watch that stuff." I turn to

Charlie. "Maybe you can find a Stephen Hawking special."

"Okay. Cool," he says, and turns on the TV.

There's no Hawking program, but there's a gory shark documentary and then a river-monster show that's irresistible to Charlie and Evan. I don't know why guys love predators with big, nasty teeth, but they do.

Nobody tells us what we're doing here, or why, or how long we have to stay with Agent A-Hole and Agent Hemorrhoid. And I won't ask them, because I hate the fact that they have been put in charge of us, and I refuse to recognize their authority.

Evan eventually tries to make polite chitchat with them but gets only grunts and yes/no answers from them, so he gives up. Which means, once the programs with the big nasty toothy creatures are over, that he has nothing to do but snore or annoy me.

"Kari," he says in cajoling tones. "You'll have to speak to me at some point."

I raise my eyebrows and make no response.

"You know you want to," he says provocatively.

I roll my eyes.

He takes it down a notch. "You don't secretly have a crush on me?" he asks. "Because I'm irresistible, and like most American girls, you have a thing for my accent? You don't want to listen to me read the phone book all day?"

Oh. My. God.

Is he for real?

There's something self-mocking in his tone, though. And then he surprises me.

"Kari," he says. "I'm sorry for not being straight with you. I truly am."

I give him my most scathing glance. It should reduce him to ashes, or at least tears.

So he gives up on me and waggles his eyebrows at Charlie.

"She wants to kiss me all over, doesn't she?"

Charlie starts to giggle, and this is the last straw.

"Quiet, you!" I say to my brother.

"I think you like him," Charlie says. He giggles some more.

Aaaargh! I jump off the bed and stand over them, my arms folded across my chest. "I do not like him," I retort. "In fact, I loathe him. There is something *very* wrong with him."

Evan is laughing now too.

"You have a personality disorder!" I fume. "Not to mention the fact that you are dishonest, two-faced, jerky, and . . . and . . . *heinous*!"

"That rhymes with anus." Charlie chortles with seven-year-old glee.

"So it does, my man," Evan concurs.

"He is not your man!" I yell.

Charlie shrinks back.

Evan inclines his head.

"Charlie, I'm sorry," I say, horrified that my brother would recoil from me. "But this guy is not cool. He's not at all nice. He's a total snake, and he's not your buddy. He's a traitor!"

"Like they're saying about Mom and Dad?" Charlie asks.

"Worse. Mom and Dad are good people who are only doing their jobs. Evan has been spying on his friends for fun. He's not who he says he is."

Charlie looks at Evan dubiously and scoots off the bed. He comes to mine instead, and crawls up on it.

Is it my imagination, or does Evan look hurt by this?

"He followed me to a Starbucks—"

"Not true. I followed *Rita* to the Starbucks," Evan corrects me.

"—and listened to my conversation. Then he followed me to the track field at Kennedy and—"

"Rita. I tracked Rita there."

"Whatever! He hid somewhere and listened to our conversation there, too. And then he uncoiled himself from his hiding spot and slithered out and forced us to let him in on the Langley deal to find Mom, and probably betrayed us and got us caught."

"Completely untrue," Evan says.

One of my mom's sayings pops into my head. *The best liars are the ones who actually convince themselves in the process.*

"I don't think you know the difference between truth and lies anymore," I tell him. "Because you *are* a walking lie."

"Whew." Evan shakes his head. "You're tough."

"Should I go easy on you? On a spy and a snake?"

"Look, if you want to call me a spy, fine. But I am not a snake. And I'm not a traitor."

"Then what are you?" I toss at him.

"I'm an agent," he says. "Just like your parents. So give me a break, okay?"

That silences me.

I turn on my heel and go into the bathroom, where I rip off the fake zit and scrub off all the horrible makeup that

Lacey applied to my face. Relieved to be me again, I swish some of the complimentary mouthwash through my teeth and resign myself to sleeping in my clothes, if I sleep at all. Then I stomp back out to the bed, turn out the bedside lamp, and crawl under the covers. Charlie is already fading.

As I close my eyes and feign unconsciousness, it occurs to me that I may not like Evan, but I need him on my side, and by tearing him a new one, I'm sabotaging that possibility.

I resolve to be nicer—in the morning.

"Sweet dreams, Kari." Evan turns off his own bedside lamp and then does a belly flop on the other bed.

"Butthead," I mutter into my pillow. After all, it's not morning yet.

Evan sighs. "I suppose I deserve that."

He absolutely does. And I spitefully wish Agent A-hole severe back pain and a horrendous crick in her neck and Agent Hemorrhoid a night of burning agony sitting upright in his chair.

In the morning I'm shocked to find that I've somehow slept, since I open my eyes and, for a moment, can't remember where I am.

Then I see Evan's sheet-creased face in the bed opposite mine. Ugh.

Charlie is snoring softly next to me.

The two agents are still at the table, looking weary and bad tempered. Ha.

Evan somehow senses that I'm awake. He squints and lifts his head from the pillow, and I have to laugh at his classic case of bedhead. For the first time ever, he doesn't look like some displaced blue blood who got on the wrong plane to America. He sits up, runs a hand sheepishly through his hair, and grimaces at me. "Good morning," he manages to say, around a yawn.

"That's debatable." I sit up in bed and give the agents the hairy eyeball. "So, you're making us pancakes and bacon, right?"

Agent A-hole looks up from her iPad. "Yeah, I'll get right on that."

"I'd like mine extra crispy, but not burnt. And blueberries in the pancakes. Lots of butter and syrup."

"Would you listen to her?" A-hole says to Hemorrhoid.

"I'm trying not to."

"I want chocolate milk," says Charlie, sitting up and rubbing his eyes.

"And would you like that served in a crystal goblet, young sir?" Hemorrhoid asks.

"Yep. With a straw." Charlie grins, enjoying the game.

"Oh, of course." He rolls his eyes at Agent A-hole and returns his attention to his laptop.

I get out of bed. "Well, it's been a real pleasure having this slumber party with you fun Feds. I'm going to take a shower and then leave."

"Siddown, kid," is all Agent A-hole says.

"How long are you going to keep us here? *Against our will.*"

"Until we get orders to release you," Hemorrhoid snaps.

I get in their faces. "This is unconstitutional. We have rights. We're innocent until proven guilty—"

"Your parents are guilty as sin, and you're minors in protective custody," A-hole growls.

"They're not!" I put my hands on my hips. "You're jumping to the same stupid conclusions that everyone else is."

The agents snort.

"The bottom line," I say to everyone, "is that my parents are loyal U.S. citizens, not double agents. They've somehow been framed, and they need help to prove that."

Evan nods. "Fair enough."

"What they do not need," I continue, looking at Agent A-hole and Agent Hemorrhoid, "is for idiots to jump to conclusions, decide they're guilty, and throw the book at them."

Agent A. and Agent H. ignore me. Agent H. shifts in his seat again, probably wishing for some Preparation H. Agent A. reaches into her soft-sided briefcase and pulls out a ChapStick.

After all, they think I'm just a misguided kid.

I glower at them.

What I need is an adult who will actually help me, but they seem to be in short supply.

Where is Aunt Sophie, by the way? Why hasn't she called me back?

Maybe she accidentally deleted my message.

Or there was a glitch in phone service, and the message never even made it to her in-box.

I guess it's possible that she lost her phone while on assignment, but I'm pretty sure she should be back by now from her latest trip.

If I can just get out of here and get to a phone, I know she'll help me.

"Evan," I whisper. "Evan!"

He turns his head.

I place a finger over my lips and jerk my head in the direction of our Agency babysitters. Then I lean really close to Charlie and tell him to do something to keep them busy. He nods.

"I'm hungry!" Charlie wails.

When he gets no immediate reaction, he howls it. "My stomach is eating itself," he complains. "I have to have food, or I'm going to get really sick and it will be all your fault." He glares at Agent A-hole.

"What, d'you think I'm your mommy?" she says rudely.

I am briefly distracted by the thought that my foot would look good planted in the middle of her face, but I let Charlie handle it.

"No, but I want breakfast," he whines. "Where's the room service menu?"

While he's got them annoyed and distracted, I whisper, "Evan, I need your help."

"Wait, what happened to me being a turd in your personal punch bowl? A traitor? A snake?"

"Come on, Evan. Don't do this."

"*Heinous*, you called me."

"Look, you can't deny that you tricked me. All of us."

He shrugs. "Okay."

"And you spied on us. And lied to us."

He exhales. "Yes. Sorry."

"Worse, you stole my first kiss ever, and I was saving it for someone else!"

He blinks. "You'd never kissed a guy?"

"No."

"What's wrong with you?"

"Nothing!"

"Haven't you ever had a boyfriend?"

"Leave me alone."

"What, you've never even played spin the bottle?"

"Could you please stop making me feel like a freak of nature?"

"But you are. What girl of sixteen has never kissed someone?"

"Evan!"

"Okay, okay. Fine."

"So will you help me? Get out of here?"

He stares moodily at me. "Who's the guy?"

"What guy?"

"The one you were saving your first kiss for?"

"None of your business. It doesn't matter, now that you've shoplifted it."

"*Shoplifted?*" His eyebrows rise into his hair.

"Yes! You're worse than Lacey Carson."

Evan is appalled.

"At least she can give back the merchandise. You can't give me back my first kiss, you jerk."

He squirms. "Look . . . Kari . . . I had no idea. You're a beautiful girl. I assumed that you'd been kissing boys since you were ten."

"So now you're calling me a ho?"

"*No.*" He throws up his hands. "Why can't I say or do anything right around you?"

I wave this issue away. "Evan. Just help me get out of here. I have to clear my parents' names. Can you understand that?"

He swallows. Looks as if he's seen a ghost—how weird. I realize that I know nothing about Evan Kincaid or his background. Just that he's a displaced Brit who's infiltrated my American school.

After a long moment Evan nods. "I'll help you. If you'll agree to take some advice. Don't go off half-cocked. And there is one other condition."

"What?" I ask impatiently.

"Charlie will have to stay here as collateral—so that I know you'll behave."

Chapter Eighteen

I balk at leaving Charlie in the care of Agents Brown and Smith, aka. A-hole and Hemorrhoid. What if something goes wrong and I have to go into hiding? Live in a gutter or a shed or a doghouse for a while?

Oh, and you'd want Charlie with you for that? My conscience attacks me.

This isn't medieval times. They're not going to stretch my little brother on the rack or tear out his toenails or starve him to death.

But they will try to use him to force me to toe the line.

I debate the question back and forth with myself.

The agents are grudgingly ordering Charlie Belgian waffles with strawberries and chocolate milk with a straw—evidence that they're not going to mistreat him.

They ask me if I want anything. I shake my head.

Evan tells them he'd like a pint of ale. They laugh at that. Then they order for themselves.

"Okay," I whisper to Evan. "But you harm a hair on his head . . ."

"Do I look like a child abuser? Really?"

"They come in all shapes and sizes, Kincaid."

"True," Evan muses. "However, you don't have to worry about me, since I won't be babysitting your brother. I'll be coming with you."

"No. Not going to happen."

"What's all the whispering over there?" Agent A-hole gripes.

"None of your business." I cast an irritated glance at her.

"Yeah? How'd you like me to gag you, Miss Smart-Mouth?"

"You'd get off on that, wouldn't you?" I retort.

She rolls her eyes and turns her back to us, staring out the window.

I turn back to Evan and say under my breath, "You are not coming with me."

He folds his arms across his chest. "Fine. Then as you're trying to give the agents the slip, I'll be sure to point out to them exactly what you're about."

"You wouldn't!"

"Try me." Evan's jaw is stubborn, and his mouth is set in a mulish line. He's not kidding.

I hate Evan Kincaid more than ever.

"You're despicable."

"Yes." He's completely unfazed. "What's your point?"

Clearly, I'm stuck with his company if I want to get out of here and find Sophie.

I turn to Charlie and whisper in his ear. "Evan and I need to go do something. You okay with staying here for a bit? With the agents?"

He scrunches up his face. "Do I have to?"

"It would be really helpful, and Mom and Dad would appreciate your cooperation."

He chews on his lip and pushes up his horn-rims. He evaluates Evan. "So he's not a snake or a traitor?"

The unspoken implication is that if he were, I wouldn't leave with him.

"No," I say, defeated. "He's all right."

Evan smiles triumphantly.

"Well . . . okay then. I guess."

"Thank you." I say it in heartfelt tones.

Evan nods. "Charlie. You are the man of the hour."

"I am?" He looks pleased.

"Yup." I ruffle his hair. "Now, how about you make another distraction, so we can get out of here and prove our parents are innocent? I swear that no matter what happens, I will come back for you. Okay?"

He nods. His eyes sparkle, and I realize that he's enjoying this. It's a different role than his usual "child genius" one, and he's reveling in it.

I blow him a kiss.

Charlie winks. Then he gets up and goes into the bathroom.

Within seconds, he's screaming murder. "*Aaaaggghhhhhhhh!*"

At the first howl the agents' heads come up. Hemorrhoid goes running into the bathroom. Evan and I jump up too.

We run to the open door.

Reluctantly A-hole follows us.

Charlie is lying on the floor, rolling as if he's in agony. He shrieks again and then convulses.

"What's wrong with him?" A-hole asks urgently.

"Oh my God. Oh my God!" Evan says.

"I don't know! I'll call 911!" I yell, and push her into the bathroom. "Do something!"

Both agents kneel over Charlie.

He's holding his breath and turning blue. He's an expert—he used to do this as a small child in order to get his way.

The agents are horrified. Hemorrhoid lays his ear to Charlie's chest, and A-hole grabs his wrist to take his pulse.

Evan and I back out. Then we quietly close the bathroom door, wedge a chair under the knob, and shrug into their jackets, which they've left hung over their chairs. I twist my hair up and secure it with a pen so that I'll look older if anyone takes a casual glance at a security camera—after all, this is an Agency safe hotel. There will definitely be surveillance.

Hats off to Charlie. In seconds we've made our escape from the room.

The hallway outside the room is empty, but I'm conscious of the security cameras as we force ourselves to walk calmly and not run. Oh, how I wish I had one of Rita's laser devices to blind the stupid things—or one of her jammers.

I nudge Evan and glance toward the little "eyes in the sky."

He nods and leans down to whisper, "Best to just let them run. Anything we do to black out the picture or create static will only attract attention."

"Yeah."

"Brace yourself—I'm betting there are guards in the lobby."

We come to the elevator and push the down button.

Unfortunately, when the doors slide open, there's a surprise inside: Gray Gary. And he's got a gun that he doesn't hesitate to pull.

"Put it on the floor," Evan says, his tone deadly.

Is he nuts?

"Or I'll shoot first."

Evan's got his right hand inside the pocket of Agent Hemorrhoid's blazer and there's a big, hard bulge there.

Gary hesitates.

"You want to be prosecuted for shooting two minors? Do it!" Evan barks.

Gary swears under his breath, then lays the gun on the floor of the elevator and puts his hands up in surrender.

"On your knees," Evan orders.

Gary obeys.

I dart forward, grab the gun, and smash the butt of it down on the back of his skull. The guy drops like a stone, his eyes rolling back in his head. Thank God there's no camera in this elevator.

"Congratulations," Evan says to Gary's prone form. "You've just been held up by an EpiPen." He pulls it out of his pocket to show me, and I have to laugh.

"You're good," I admit.

He grins. "I know."

The awesome thing is that we now have a gun, which helps us a lot with getting out of the hotel. It intimidates the guard at the back door enough that we're able to gag him and cuff him—with his own bracelets—to his chair.

What can I say? Bullets are the spice of life.

Evan's hot-wiring skills are every bit as good as my own, and I'm forced to compliment him as we borrow the agents' car—the black, government-issued Crown Vic we arrived here in last night.

I give him directions to my house so that I can raid my mom's closet for a new disguise.

"Is it wise for us to go to your house?" Evan asks. "Won't the Agency have it under surveillance?"

"I doubt it," I say after a moment's reflection. "They'd have watched it for the first couple of days, but after that? When nobody in our family showed up? Why waste the manpower?"

Evan concedes that I may be right, but we'll have to be careful.

"We need to call my Aunt Sophie," I tell him. "She'll help us." Evan starts to ask me just who Sophie is, but I tell him it's my turn to ask him questions.

What brought his parents over to the U.S.? What do they do?

I guess I just assumed that Evan had parents, like

everyone else at Kennedy Prep, but this turns out not to be the case.

He clears his throat. "I live with . . . a woman."

A woman? I turn and stare at him. "What do you mean? You're—I mean—um. Are you . . . her boy toy?"

"Good God, no!" he says, laughing.

"Well, I guess it's no big deal if you are. It explains the snooty clothes—"

"Snooty clothes?" he chokes.

"Well, tailored—"

"It's no crime to wear clothes that actually fit. That doesn't mean I'm some kind of kept man!"

"Okay, okay. I believe you."

"My parents are dead," he finally says, after a long pause. "I live with Agent Rebecca Morrow and her husband Stefan and daughter Abby. I've been in the Interpol program since I was thirteen, so I go where they tell me to go."

"Thirteen?" I repeat.

He nods.

"Can I ask . . . not to be nosy, but what happened to your parents, Evan?" Up to now I've been under the delusion that there's nothing worse than having people think your parents are traitors to their country. But I have to admit that having your parents be dead trumps that.

"My mom—" Evan takes a corner way too fast, and then accelerates through the turn. "My mom was killed in a hostage situation when I was ten. She was working as a negotiator. She agreed to go into a flat if they'd release a little girl in exchange for her.

"Then the top brass sent in a CO19 unit—what you

would call a SWAT team here—and the bad guys told them to back the hell off, or they'd start shooting people. The CO19 guys didn't, and so the bastards grabbed my mother and put a bullet through her head, then shoved her out the front door of the apartment. If their bullet hadn't killed her, the rain of bullets by the cops, as she fell out the door, would have."

I find that it's hard to breathe. Evan takes another corner, faster than the first. "And your dad?" I venture after a few moments.

"Three years later. Shot in a drug raid. He was an undercover narcotics officer. Oddly enough, he too was accused of being a double agent, Kari. But it was his handler. Nice, eh?"

"So that's why you got that funny look on your face back in the hotel room. You understand my need to clear my parents' names."

"Yes," Evan says. "More than most."

We drive in silence for a while, caught in the blasted traffic that is a way of life in DC. There are more cars than politicians, lobbyists, and diplomats, and more of those than there are trees.

"So you don't have aunts or uncles or grand—"

"No," Evan says. "Nobody. You'd think that given the circumstances, especially after my mum died, that my dad would have chosen something less risky to do for a living. But he wasn't cut out for anything else."

"I'm sorry," I tell him. I feel awful now for all the terrible things I've said to him. His mouth twists. "Don't go all soft on me now, Shrew."

"I'm not—I'm just saying—"

"I don't want your bloody pity," he says, his voice almost a snarl. "So save it."

"There's a difference between pity and an apology, dickhead!"

"That's better," Evan tells me. "That's my girl."

I open my mouth to tell him that I'm so not his girl, but right then he makes the turn—again at warp speed, so that I fall against him—onto my street. And right there, opposite our house, I see a familiar car leaving.

"That's Sophie's car!" I say.

"That stunning blonde is Sophie?" Evan asks.

"Yeah. That was Auntie Soph all right. Though I don't know what she was doing at our house with nobody home."

"Does she have a key?"

"Of course. Sophie's like Mom's little sister. She was probably looking for me. I'll call her once we get inside." I reach for my cell phone before I remember it's been confiscated.

"And you don't think she stopped by for popcorn and a solitary movie?"

Evan nods. "At least our question is answered—it doesn't look as if anyone from the Agency is here, or they would have taken her down."

I exhale. "That's a relief."

Evan backs the car into the driveway so no one can see the license plate, and then shuts off the engine.

The sudden silence is a little eerie, but it feels good to be home.

Chapter Nineteen

Our house is a neat brick Colonial with a black door and shutters. It looks the same as always, with no indication that the lives of its inhabitants have been turned upside down. The dogwood tree still shades the front yard, and Mom's window boxes still bloom with fake red impatiens. She tried planting real ones, but she's gone too much to keep up with them, and Charlie and I forget to water them.

Evan looks around once we're inside, and I try to see the place through his eyes, which is hard because I've lived here so long that I barely notice the furnishings anymore: hardwood floors, forgettable beige furniture—and on the walls—things from every corner of the world. There are Russian icons, Asian painted screens, Turkish footstools, and Persian rugs.

My favorite piece in the house was painted right here in

the good ol' US of A, though. It's a portrait of us—Mom, Dad, me, and Charlie—that hangs over the brick fireplace, done just two years ago when my brother was five. We are the picture of the perfect American family. I stare at that painting a lot when Mom and Dad are traveling. It's my source of comfort, however stupid that might sound.

I tell myself to focus, to move quickly, to come up with another persona.

I end up bypassing Mom's closet. Since I've already done the office manager disguise, and there's no way I'll pass as an old lady without someone really good to do my makeup (ha!—that would not be me), I decide that it's easier if I dress as a boy.

I tuck my hair up into an old Redskins cap of my dad's and pull on a pair of gray, unisex sweatpants. A sloppy long-sleeved tee, sneakers, and a Windbreaker complete the illusion—and my flat chest and athletic frame help too.

I add a pair of my dad's aviator sunglasses and almost do a cheer that I don't have to mess with eye shadow or mascara or lipstick.

"Not bad," Evan has to admit.

Because we can't be sure the house phone isn't bugged, we get into the car and call Sophie from his cell phone, which somehow he's managed to snag back from the agents—I don't ask how. All I know is that it's constantly ringing or pinging, and he's constantly pressing the mute button and ignoring it.

Sophie answers on the very first ring.

"Sophie, it's me, Kari."

"Kari!" she exclaims. "Are you okay? What about Charlie? Where are you?"

"Did you get my message?" I ask her.

"I just got it. I was about to call you—I only flew back into National from a shoot in Málaga, Spain, this morning. What's going on?"

"Soph, I don't want to get into it over the phone because it's not safe. There are people looking for me, people who want to kidnap me. Meet me at our usual spot in two hours, okay?"

"But—" She breaks off.

"All the kids in the city will be out of school by then, so we won't be so noticeable. We'll blend into the crowd."

"Okay. I'll meet you there."

"Great. Thanks. See you soon." I hang up.

"Usual spot?" queries Evan. "Where is that? How well do you know this woman? Who is she, exactly? And is it safe to meet her?"

"I've known Sophie forever. Since I was little. My mom was her alumna mentor in college, and they're sorority sisters, and she used to babysit for me and Charlie. Sophie is like family to us."

Evan seems reassured.

I tell him to go to a nearby shopping mall, and, predictably, he's not thrilled.

"Retail hell twice in one week—God save me. Can't we meet this woman somewhere else?"

"No. This is our usual spot to meet and talk and catch up with each other."

He shudders. "Girls and their shopping. Spare me!"

"You didn't seem to mind Victoria's Secret," I say acidly.

"That's different."

I snort.

"You're the one who insisted on forcing your company on me, so don't complain now," I tell him. "Be nice—or I'll tell Sophie to force you into a shoe warehouse."

Evan blanches with horror, to my satisfaction.

We park and make our way inside to a large fountain in the center of the mall. Sure enough, there's gorgeous, blond Sophie, dressed in her habitual black—pacing back and forth and clearly on edge. That's not like her. Her tussle of gold and silver hair is uncharacteristically messy, and the navy eyeliner under her gray eyes is smudged. She looks tired—but still impossibly glamorous, with huge diamond studs sparkling in her ears.

I walk right up to her, but it takes her a minute to recognize me under the baseball cap, and she's not expecting Evan.

"Kari!" She holds open her arms, and I step into them and it feels so good. She smells of leather and patchouli. My nose starts to itch immediately, because of the patchouli.

I introduce Evan as a schoolmate, nothing more.

She appraises him openly, female to male, not at all shy about it. It makes me uncomfortable.

"Shall I show you my teeth?" he asks, with a charming little wink.

She laughs out loud. "My, this one's got a mouth on him, Kari. Though I rather like that in a man." She smiles at him, then at me, her smoky-mauve lipstick gleaming under the mall's fluorescent lighting. "How've you been, honey?" She grabs my wrist. "And is that a new charm?"

"Not great, actually." I tug my wrist free. "I'll show the charm to you later. Soph, I'm in trouble."

Her eyebrows draw together. She almost looks mad or impatient for a second, but she must just be exhausted from her trip.

The splash of the fountain and the echoes of hundreds of voices make it hard to converse, but equally hard for anyone to overhear what we're saying, so it's the perfect place for this conversation. I explain about my missing dad and say my mom is missing too. I don't get into the details, since Sophie doesn't know what they truly do for a living.

"And Charlie?" she asks, concerned.

"He's safe."

"Safe where?" Sophie's eyebrows rise. "Or should I not ask?"

"No, probably not." My mouth twists. I struggle with how much to say, and she clearly senses that.

"Look, honey . . . I've known for a while that Cal and Irene don't have what you'd call regular desk jobs. I know that they're with the Agency. I know they're spies."

I gape at her. "You do?"

She nods.

"*How* do you know that?"

She shifts from foot to foot, then shrugs. "Over the years I've connected the dots. And when I told Irene what my instincts said to me, she didn't deny it. But she didn't elaborate, either. So I don't know any specifics."

I don't know exactly how to proceed. Sophie's eyes are sympathetic, and she puts her hands on my shoulders. "Kari. Sweetheart. How can I help?"

My eyes fill with tears. This woman has been like a second mother to me. She has come to school plays and Girl Scout activities, given baths and made brownies; she's been camping with us and even invented a special s'more for my little brother, with grape jelly added to it, called the Charlie.

"Kari, honey, talk to me. Let me know what I can do to help you."

I take a deep breath; then I take a big chance. This is the Sophie I know and love, and not some awful stranger. "Okay. We do need all the help we can get."

Evan shoots me a "What, are you an imbecile?" glare, but I'm in charge here, and this is my call. So I ignore him.

"For right now, since I'm still officially a missing person, let's go back to the house and out of the public."

Sophie nods. "Makes sense."

"What if the house is under surveillance?" Evan asks pointedly. "What if it's bugged?" He's clearly trying to steer me away from this course of action.

"If so, then Agency people would have followed us here and picked us up already. But we can check again before we go in. You and Sophie can drive, and I'll keep my head down until we know if anyone's there or not."

"Fine. Whatever." He still seems pissed—but it's probably just because he wants to be in charge and call all the shots. Tough.

I decide to leave the agents' car in the mall parking lot. It's a liability, since they'll be looking for it. So we all pile into Sophie's.

I lie down on Sophie's backseat for the duration of the ride.

"Well, here we are," she says, as she pulls up to the house. "No sign of anyone."

"There could be an entire SWAT team hiding in the shrubbery, and you'd never know it," Evan remarks.

"Well, you're more than welcome to get out and beat around the bushes," I snark at him. "And while you're at it, would you please, for the love of God, answer your cell phone or put it on vibrate? The stupid thing hasn't stopped ringing since we left the hotel."

"What can I say? I'm a popular guy."

"Say hello! 'Cause I'm ready to stomp on it."

"There's that violent streak again that I love." But Evan gets out of the car and walks into the yard, peering into the bushes and then heading for the back garden. I hate to admit it, but he could be right—a whole battalion could be stationed there, and we wouldn't have a clue until it was too late.

A few moments later he returns through the gate on the other side of the yard, and gives us a thumbs-up while talking to someone on his phone.

Sophie cuts the engine and we go inside. Evan stays in the yard.

We sit down on the couch in front of the fireplace and there's an awkward silence. Sophie glances up at the family portrait and then looks away. Is it my imagination, or does a fleeting sneer cross her face?

I decide it's my imagination, because she breaks the silence by saying, "Kari, this must be really hard on you. I'm so sorry."

I shrug. "It's not like it's your fault."

"Well, of course not, but that doesn't mean that I can't feel for you, honey. I—" She breaks off and shakes her head.

"What?" I ask anxiously.

"Well, I always did question why Cal and Irene would stay in a profession with such risks when they had two beautiful children who depended on them."

"It's what they do," I say quietly. "They do it for the country, just like anyone in the military. They protect our freedoms, our way of life."

Sophie pats my knee. "Of course. Of course. You must be proud of them."

"I am. But I don't know how to clear their names. I need your help, Soph. You're an international journalist. You have contacts, right?"

"I am a photographer," she corrects me.

"But you sell to big magazines—"

She raises her eyebrows. "So?"

"Well, surely one of them would publish an article, or—" I break off, because her expression is not encouraging.

"Kari, honey, *National Geographic* isn't going to run an ad or an exposé for you on the Agency."

"But—"

"I can't help you that way. I can only help you in terms of . . . ," she seemed to struggle, "moral support."

"I don't need moral support! I need an action plan!"

She shakes her head. "All you can do is wait."

I want to scream. Wait? For what? For everything *else* to go wrong? I jump up and begin to pace, while another long pause stretches between me and Sophie, until finally, she changes the subject, probably hoping to distract me and calm me down.

"You've got your charm bracelet on, I see."

"Always."

"So, show me the new charm," she says. "What is it? Where's it from?"

"It's Bran Castle, Dracula's home. From Romania."

"Ooooh," Sophie says, with a delicious shiver. "Can I see it?"

Sophie always wants to examine the little details on the new charms my parents send to me. "Sure." I slip off the bracelet, undo the clasp on the Bran's Castle charm, and hand it to her.

She oohs and ahs over the tiny etched windows and doors, the proud little crenellated tower.

I notice that her lips aren't pale pink like they always have been since I can remember. "Hey, Soph? Did you change your lip color? It seems darker."

She looks up at me. "Oh!" She laughs airily. "Do you like it? I wanted to try something new. I've been wearing the same old thing for the last five years and got sick of it."

My nose starts to itch. Badly. "Yeah, it's nice," I tell her.

"I lost my last tube of the other one when I was on assignment in Milan a few months ago, and since Lancôme's discontinued the shade, I bought a different one."

"Looks good." I smile at her. "It's a really natural-looking color."

"The other one was more glam," she says. "But 'natural' is in style." She looks me over. "But not *that* natural, honey."

"I'm disguised as a boy!" I remind her.

She sighs. "Okay. Today you get a pass, but, Kari, how are you ever going to catch a guy if you don't wear some makeup and work at being feminine?"

I stick out my tongue at her. "Catch a guy? Like with a net? That's so 1950s."

I hate to admit it, but Soph occasionally makes me feel like Lacey does. Not that she means to.

"Case in point—your Evan, out there."

I make a face. "He's so not *my* Evan."

"Well, a little eyeliner and mascara could make him yours."

"Oh, very true," he says, winking from the doorway.

Startled, Sophie drops the charm.

I spring two feet off the sofa, in absolute horror. How is it, *why* is it, that this guy is witness to my *every* humiliation? Or the cause of it?

"But without eyeliner and mascara?" He shakes his head. "Not a chance. Not a chance in hell. Simply revolting."

Revolting? I think he's teasing, but I'm not sure.

Sophie laughs like a loon.

All I can think to do is stick my head under the cocktail table to retrieve the charm she dropped.

I guess Sophie reaches for it at the same time, because our heads bang together. "Ow!" I sit up and rub my head. Then I bend down and stretch my hand out for the little charm, but Sophie pounces on it and scrabbles it away from me. I sit up and stare at her, and she shrugs.

"Sorry. Guess I've had too much coffee today!" She takes my bracelet, reattaches the charm to it, and then hands it over to me.

"So," says Evan, with a polite smile. "Should I run out for mascara then, Kari? Would you like black or brown?"

I hate him.

Hate. Hate. Hate.

Where is Luke? Why can't I be with him, instead?

God is cruel.

Chapter Twenty

I notice that Sophie keeps looking at her watch. "Do you have a hot date?" I ask. Maybe it's petty, but I'm a little hurt that here I am, in the biggest trouble of my life, and she's acting pressed for time.

"No, no," she says, standing up. "But I should probably get going. I have a deadline."

I stare at her. "You have a deadline," I repeat.

"Well. Yes. Not that it's more important than your, um, situation here. I just don't see quite how I can help. . . ." Her voice trails off at my expression.

It's almost dinnertime, and my stomach growls audibly.

"Oh, poor Kari," Soph says, checking her watch again. "*That's* how I can help. Why don't I run and pick up some takeout for supper?"

Sophie is dying to leave the house for some reason.

"No," Evan says decisively. "We all need to stick together. For safety's sake."

I cast a puzzled frown in his direction. Why would Soph be in any danger?

"You never know—Sophie could be a target because of her close association with the family."

It's definitely not my imagination that she goes pale. And shifts her weight from one foot to the other. And swallows.

"Soph? You okay?" I ask.

"Of course. Don't be silly. And I think you're worrying unnecessarily, Evan. Just because I'm a friend of the family doesn't mean I have *anything* to do with Cal and Irene's work. Nothing at all."

Weirdly enough, my nose starts to itch again.

Evan tilts his head and evaluates her. He opens his mouth to say something, but his phone rings again, and he walks into another room to take the call.

"*What?* You're kidding," we hear him say. "He's gone? She is too?"

Immediately my mind jumps to Charlie, and the blood in my veins turns to ice. Oh my God. Has someone kidnapped him? I shouldn't have left him at the hotel!

Evan says, "Yes, ma'am. I understand. Yes." He hangs up and walks in, just as I get up to run into the dining room, where he's been talking.

"Kari, you may want to sit down for this." His face is deadly serious.

"Oh, Jesus." My knees become rubber and I collapse onto the sofa, right in the exact spot I was in before. "What is it? Please tell me it's not Charlie. . . ."

"He's missing." Evan's voice breaks. Weird—is it possible that he's gotten so attached to my little brother in such a short amount of time? "They think that your parents took him though. Your mom's cell is also empty, and the agents who were guarding her, as well as the ones who were with Charlie, have been knocked out and tied up."

I'm half-elated—my mom's escaped—and half-horrified. *When all else fails, resort to violence.* If it is my parents, then this makes them fugitives from the law. Everyone will be looking—

My train of thought is broken as Sophie jumps over the coffee table and hurtles for the front door. What the hell?

Evan goes flying after her and tackles her two feet short of it. "Where do you think you're going?" he asks.

"Get off me!" she yells.

I can barely register what I'm seeing as Sophie bucks and flails to get out from under him, unsuccessfully. Then she twists so that she's facing him and tries to drive her thumbs up into his eye sockets. Evan attempts to grab her wrists, but she tears one out of his grasp and drives a knee up into his gut.

I'm in shock. *What* is going on?

Something tiny and silver streaks through the air and falls onto the hardwood floor near the sofa with a bounce. I look down at it and see my Bran Castle charm. But that's impossible, because the one on my bracelet is still attached. I turn it to make sure.

I reach down to pick up the extra charm and freeze. *This* is my charm. I can tell because there's a little fleck of green paint just below the crenellated tower. The green paint from my art class a couple of days ago.

"Kari, what is it?" Evan calls.

I turn to tell him, just as Sophie reaches up to grab one of the heavy brass candlesticks on the foyer table by the front door. I scream a warning too late as she brings the base of it down on his temple.

Evan crumples under her.

Oh, God. I hope Evan's okay. Please let him be okay . . .

Sophie launches herself at me, a diamond-studded ninja. "Give me that!"

My martial arts training and my adrenaline kick in at the same time, and when she goes to punch me, I clamp down hard on her fist and use it to twist her arm backward unnaturally. Then I knee her in the stomach. She shrieks and doubles over.

"Why do you want the charm?" I demand.

She drives her head forward, aiming for my gut, but I sidestep, and she plows her skull right into the wall. Not so smart.

"Give it to me!" she screams, when she can stand upright again.

"No. What's it to you?"

"Give me the damn charm!" she bellows, and comes for me again.

But she's not trained as well as I am, and she's already tired from fighting with Evan. I clamp onto her left wrist and elbow this time and flip her. She lands on her back on the hardwood floor, the wind knocked out of her.

I hold the charm up to my mouth. "Tell me why you

want it, Sophie, or I'll swallow it. Then you'll have to wait a day or two, and you'll have a nasty time locating it."

"No! No!" She manages, after gasping for air. "Don't do that."

I hear a noise outside. A car door? Crap! The Agency's found us.

Sophie takes instant advantage of my distraction. She rolls over, onto Evan, and snatches something from the back of his pants. Then she vaults into a squat and smiles triumphantly, because the "something" is Gary's gun, and she's aiming it right at me.

Sophie laughs at the expression on my face. "Men. So useless, unless you want some eye candy, maybe a fat wallet, a little sausage. Or, in special circumstances like these, a weapon."

I can't even compute this. My aunt Soph, waving a gun in my face. Over a silver charm!

"Why do you want the charm, Sophie?" I ask. "Why?"

"Just hand it over, Kari. Now!"

My mind races. I think back to the lipstick in her shade, the one that Mr. Carson told me is capable of copying microchips. What else is small enough to encase a microchip?

"There's a microchip inside of that little castle," I say. "Isn't there?"

"One plus one is two," Sophie says.

"And somehow you've been copying them . . . with the tube of lip color that you 'lost' in Milan?"

"Two plus two is four," Sophie says, in the most patronizing tone imaginable. She produces a nasty little laugh.

"For God's sake, Kari. You never were very bright, but in this case, it took you long enough to do the math!"

I stare at her as if I've never seen her before. I stare at her until her features blur, and I realize that this is because tears have formed in my eyes. Tears, this time, of hurt and shock and betrayal. "How *could* you?"

She tosses her hair. "The money is fantastic, kid. Photography equipment is expensive. So are diamonds. So is world travel. I have a lifestyle to maintain."

"But . . . Sophie, you're screwing over the U.S.! You're hurting the country. Don't you care?"

"Four plus four is eight, stupid girl. I wasn't born here! I come from just outside Saint Petersburg, Russia. Why would I care about the security of the United States?"

An icy dread is growing within me, burning and freezing at the same time.

"Give me the charm," she orders again.

"Eight plus eight is sixteen," I say, my voice very quiet. "I'm doing the math now, Sophie. So you were never my friend. Never 'practically family.' You've just cultivated us and used us all of these years."

"Well, hallelujah," she mock exults. "There's some hope for you yet, girl. Why else would I hang around with a woman I despise and her malleable dolt of a husband and two snot-nosed children?"

My whole body is trembling. I'm not proud of that, but I can't help it.

I've never met this woman, the one holding a gun on me. The one now cocking the hammer. The one with the coldest, darkest, shark-gray eyes I've ever seen.

207 / TWO LIES AND A SPY

"For the last time, Karina. Give me the charm."

I throw it at her, deliberately wide, so that she'll have to take her eyes off me to locate it and pick it up. While she does that, while she's distracted, I'm going to jump her, and it will be a fight until disorientation or death.

But instead of falling for my ploy, Sophie sights down the gun, taking careful aim at my forehead. And I know with finality that I'm going to die.

"It won't hurt, Kari. You won't feel any pain," she promises.

Thanks, bitch. Thanks a lot.

And then there's an explosion of sound.

Chapter Twenty-One

Our front door implodes just as Sophie squeezes the trigger. It's my dad, who's kicked it right off the hinges, and my mom, who plows into Sophie like a rocket-propelled missile, with just as much fire and fury. I've never been so glad to see them. Ever.

Sophie's shot goes wide, and instead of embedding itself in my brain, the bullet tears into my right shoulder. At first I don't even realize it. I'm not even sure if I'm alive or dead. Could I be seeing all of this from the other side? I definitely saw a brilliant white light, that's for sure.

I suck in a breath and realize that my right shoulder hurts worse than the time I dislocated it. It's on fire and throbbing so much that tears run down my face before I even realize I'm crying.

Mom is now sitting on Sophie, her knee in the small of the psycho's back. She jerks Sophie's arms behind her and trusses her wrists together as if Soph is our Thanksgiving turkey and Mom is Rachel Ray.

If the throbbing in my shoulder were audible, it would sound like a tuba.

Dad runs toward me with a towel and a medical kit.

"This is going to hurt, kiddo," he says gruffly, and without warning he presses the towel to my shoulder. I scream—can't help it—and he claps a hard, suffocating hand over my mouth. It's so alien to me that I almost take a chunk out of his palm, and we lock eyes furiously.

"Kari . . . I'm sorry. I was afraid someone would hear."

Like the gunshot was silent?

I shake my head, then clamp my own hand down on the towel against my shoulder, which hurts beyond belief. But I stand up. *"Where's Charlie?"*

Images of him tied up or terrified or wounded flash through my mind. My voice goes an octave higher. "Where *is* he?!"

"I'm right here, Kari." He steps into the living room, all forty-two pounds and three and a half feet of him. I'm so relieved to see him, not a hair on his strawberry blond head harmed, that I almost pass out. Instead I close my eyes for a second, then blink back more tears.

"Kari?" Charlie's eyes go owl-like behind his glasses. "Kari, you're . . ." He runs for me. "Bleeding!" He throws his arms around me and starts to hyperventilate. "You can't die," he says into my stomach.

"I'm not dying, kiddo. I swear." I stroke his sweet, cowlicked head and try to swallow past a lump in my throat the size of a Volkswagen.

His little body shudders against mine, and his face is tearstained when he looks up at me. "Promise?"

I nod.

"Swear? Cross your heart and hope to—" He breaks off, disturbed by what he almost says.

"I cross my heart and swear," I say with all the reassurance I can muster. "I feel great."

I grab Charlie's hand and turn to look down at Evan's prone form on the floor. My God, I hope Sophie hasn't killed him. "But I don't think *he* does. Doc, will you check his pulse? Is he okay?"

Charlie gasps as he sees Evan, nods, lets go of my hand, and kneels next to him, solemnly placing two fingers to the side of his patient's neck.

God, I love that kid. I am so proud of the way he's keeping his head.

Dad is advancing on me with the first aid kit again. I don't resist this time as he makes me sit on the sofa, then cuts off the blood-soaked sleeve of my white T-shirt. He cleans the wound while Charlie places his ear against Evan's heart.

"He's okay." Charlie bends over him again. "He's breathing steadily."

The guy's got a thick skull. "Thanks, doc. Good deal." I release a breath I wasn't aware I was holding. "Now," I say to my parents, as Dad gently presses clean gauze to the wound in my shoulder. "What . . . how . . . where . . ."

"Dad's a hero!" Charlie announces. "He rescued Mom from the bad guys—"

Is that a scoffing noise coming from Psycho Sophie?

Even with her face pressed into our Oriental rug?

"And then they came and got me. Dad knocked out one guy with his fist and the other guy with the butt of his gun, and then Mom tied them up. Mom's real good at tying people up, did you know?"

This time there's an unmistakable snort out of Sophie.

My formerly chic and classy mom drives a fist into the vicinity of Soph's kidneys. *Ouch.*

Then Mom gets off Sophie, stands up, and brushes the beige carpet fibers off her black business slacks. "Cal," she says in close to normal tones, "are you almost done, there? We've got to go."

"Go?" Charlie asks. "We just got home."

"I know, sweetheart." Mom pastes on a smile. "But . . . we broke out of the Agency, honey. And we assaulted federal officers when we took you. So we're in trouble—and we've got to leave."

"But, Mom," I say. "This is all a big misunderstanding. You're innocent! And you went into that hotel room to rescue your *child*. You came here to ensure the safety of your *other* child. The Agency will understand."

"Kari, I know you have a lot of questions," Dad says smoothly. "But—"

"We don't have time to answer them at the moment. Let's hustle," Mom orders. "A plane is coming for us in half an hour, and the airstrip is a good forty minutes away."

"What airstrip?"

"Grab your backpacks," Mom orders.

"Really, Mom? You think we still have those, after everything we've been through? I'll go pack a bag for me and Charlie."

"No time," she says. "Come on, everyone. Get out the door and into the Suburban. Grab Sophie."

"What about Evan?"

"What about him?" Dad asks, casting a dismissive glance his way. "The Agency people will find him. I'm sure they're on their way."

"You guys, it doesn't make any sense for us to leave!" I say. "Running will just make you look guilty of something. You have to talk this out with your handlers, with your superiors at work."

Mom has a tic at the corner of her left eye. "Kari." Her voice is strained. "You've lost a lot of blood, and you're feeling weak."

True. She can always read me.

"So I know that nothing about this seems logical at the moment, but we have to leave, *now.*" Her voice rises on the last word. "We can talk everything through later, once we're on the plane."

"But—" I scratch my itchy nose.

Dad has Charlie by the elbow and is steering him toward the door.

"Stop giving me lip, young lady!" Mom snaps.

At which point I hear Evan's voice, as British and upper-crust as ever. "I beg your pardon," he says from the floor. "But why *can't* you clarify things for your daughter—and other interested parties—right now? It seems to me that Kari's got the right of it—innocent families don't normally flee the country on private jets, eh?"

"Who said anything about a private jet?" Dad growls.

Evan gingerly sits up, then raises an eyebrow and pokes his tongue into his cheek. "Oh, of course. You're taking a US

Airways flight out of Dulles, sir, going through security—with that disassembled sniper rifle in your rucksack."

Only Sophie laughs at his sarcasm.

Evan has a good eye—sure enough, Dad's backpack is lying half open on the floor, and a scope is visible. Dad's eyes narrow. Then he moves Charlie another couple of steps toward the exit.

Mom runs to the pack, scoops everything back into it, and hands it to him. Then she reaches for my arm, but I sidestep and spin away from her. "You tell me what's going on, right now. Why do we have to run?"

Nobody says a word. Nobody makes a sound.

And then simultaneously, I sneeze and Sophie lets loose with another nasty cackle.

"Kari," she says, rolling onto her side. "Once again, I gave you credit for being more intelligent."

I stare at her.

She smirks. "Think about it. Who sent you the charms with the microchips inside? Your mother and father *are* Russian spies, doll."

Silence.

The room shrieks with it, with the lack of denial from either one of my parents.

My nose no longer tickles, but I can't breathe. And clarity is cold in my mind. The chill seeps from there downward, into my neck and shoulders, down my spine . . . all the way to my feet, now frozen and rooted to the ground.

I turn my head and stare at Mom—who simply closes her eyes.

Since she has nothing to say, I look to Dad, who drags a weary hand down his face and drops Charlie's hand.

Poor Charlie looks flabbergasted; his posture's like a plush toy's with the stuffing ripped out.

"Irina," Dad grates out. "Was there a *reason* you didn't gag that woman?"

"I could ask you the same, Cal."

Irina? My mom's name is Irene.

"Nooooooooooooooooooo!" Charlie howls, and launches himself at Dad. He beats at his chest with his small fists. "You're *not* Russian spies, you're not, you're not, you're *not*!" He bursts into tears. "Tell her, Daddy! Tell her. . . ."

Dad's face is ashen. "Charlie—" He tries to put his arms around my brother.

"TELL HER!" Charlie screams, tears and spittle flying from his mouth, hitting Dad's face as he bends down to hug him.

"Charlie," Dad says. "I love you."

"Nooooo!" my brother shrieks. He throws himself down to avoid Dad's encircling arms, and when Mom rushes to him, he slaps at her knees. "I hate you!"

Charlie scrambles over to me on all fours, and I pick him up, hugging him tightly despite the agony this causes my shoulder. He sobs out his heartbreak, his disillusionment, his disgust.

Mom is trembling from head to toe, but her eyes are icy and her jaw is like granite.

Dad looks broken. Just . . . defeated.

Mom's mouth opens, and these are the words that I hear, as if from a long way off. "All right. That's enough drama. Now we're leaving."

Is she kidding? What is she smoking?

"We're not going anywhere with you," I manage to say over Charlie's tousled head. He's still weeping into my good shoulder.

My mom curses—something I've never, ever heard her do. "Kari, get moving! Cal, muscle her into the Suburban."

Evan hauls himself to his feet. "Not going to happen," he says firmly.

Like some crazed action figure, Mom takes two steps, wrenches a Sig Sauer out of her Fendi bag, and takes aim at Evan.

"Sorry, Charlie," I say, and toss him bodily onto an overstuffed love seat. I step between Mom and Evan. Her eyes widen, but even now, the gun doesn't waver. I stare into the black barrel, rather than into the eyes that have now betrayed everything I can think of: ideals, country, family, the very concept of motherhood.

She has used me, her own daughter, to pass information. She's teaching Charlie foreign languages so she can use him, too—a seven-year-old!—if she hasn't already.

"We're not going anywhere with you, *Irina*. At this point we don't even know who you people are."

"Kari, we're your parents."

"Right . . . that's why you've got a gun trained on me."

Charlie suddenly clues in and goes ballistic, screaming "No! No! No!" over and over again. He hurls himself off the sofa and crawls to me on all fours. He clings to my knees as if he's drowning and I'm a life preserver.

Mom's face crumples. She drops the Sig onto the

floor, and Evan swoops around me and kicks it toward the fireplace.

"Charlie," Mom says. "Come on, baby. You know I'd never hurt your sister. Let's go, sweetheart."

"No! I hate you! I hate you!" Charlie shrieks. "You're a liar! You're a bad person!"

Mom looks sucker punched.

"Charlie, don't speak to your mother like that," Dad says sternly. "Now, come on." He grabs my brother's arm and tries to pull him away from me. Charlie screeches. He kicks backward. Then he turns his head and sinks his teeth into Dad's hand.

"Turn him loose!" I scream simultaneously.

Dad recoils, stares down at his now bloody hand and then at his son in disbelief.

I look at my father with loathing. "He's. Not. Going. With you."

Dad's face goes blank. He backs up, walks over to Mom, puts his big hand on the back of her neck, and pushes her toward the door. "We're done here."

She blinks rapidly, then stumbles as she cranes her head to look back at us.

He drives her forward, shaking his head. "Time to go. They're minors. They'll be okay." Dad's gaze locks with mine. "We *will* come back for you."

"Don't bother." I force out the words. I'm so cold, so appalled, so . . . shell-shocked . . . that I can't access my emotions, much less process them. I just want to hurt them as much as they've hurt us.

"Kari and Charlie—" His voice breaks, and his eyes fill

with tears. "Whatever happens, please know that we love you more than anything on this earth."

"Right."

"I swear it."

My mom is sobbing now, her shoulders shaking. She evidently can't speak. She blows a wet, tearful kiss at us.

Dad shoves her out the door and into the Suburban. Then he comes back for hog-tied Sophie, who's lost a lot of her bravado and now seems actively scared.

"Kari, don't let them take me!" she begs. "They'll kill me . . ."

"You," I say slowly, "*disgust* me. I could care less what happens to you. Or them."

"Kari!" she pleads.

But I don't answer, and my father shoves a rag into her mouth.

My last image is of my dad hoisting her up by the rope that connects her bound hands to her bound feet. He grunts and walks out with her, as if she's a heavy stack of old newspapers he's carting to the curb.

I stare stonily, unforgiving, as the door closes behind them. I feel weathered and petrified, a thousand years old. I sway on my feet and dimly note the pain still in my shoulder.

It's nothing compared to the ache in my heart, the suffocating bile rising in my throat, the nausea invading my stomach.

My parents are Russian spies? *Traitors?*

I'm so cold.

So very cold.

And then I'm falling, but I can't be bothered to even flail my arms. It's just too much effort, and I'd have to care—which I'm beyond doing.

Charlie yells something.

I hear footsteps running toward me—Evan's?

Then everything goes black.

Chapter Twenty-Two

"Wake up, Shrew," Evan's voice pleads with me. "C'mon. Wake up and say something rude. Please."

I hear the words as if from a long way off.

I'm not sure where I am, but the air smells familiar . . . like wood and old rugs and espresso and cinnamon. Oh, that's it. I'm home. It smells like home.

Except there's something wrong.

I don't want to be here.

Home is now a bad place, for some reason. Can't remember why . . .

"For the love of God, Karina, I'm begging you," Evan says. "Insult me!"

Ha. That one's easy.

"Asshole," I mumble.

"Yes! Brilliant! Charlie, she's awake!"

"You said a bad word," Charlie's voice says.

I try to nod, but my head won't move. I think it's nailed to the floor.

"Worse," Evan prompts. "Come on, Kari. Call me something worse. Stay with us."

I really wish my head wasn't nailed to the floor, because it would work better if I could move it. What's worse than "asshole"? Hmmm.

Charlie evidently doesn't approve. "Potty-mouth!"

"Charlie, little man. Give us a bit of a break here. I'm trying to keep your sister conscious, understand?"

"Oh."

"Bloody hell!" Evan's voice sounds agonized. "I was assigned to protect her, and I've let this happen—*damn it!*"

Huh? "Wh-what do you mean?" I manage to ask.

"Kari, I wasn't spying on you—or your parents—all this time. I was supposed to protect you, look out for you—" His voice actually breaks.

I absorb this for a few moments. Wow. "Ha," I say. "What if you'd . . . messed up . . . your hair?"

He chuckles weakly.

I'm falling asleep again, which feels really good, when chaos erupts all around us. I hear heavy trucks or vans squeal up outside, then shouts of "Agency! Hands up!" and dozens of boots hit the hardwood floors and thunder around.

"Man down!" yells Evan. "Woman, I should say."

"911 en route," Charlie announces.

"What happened?" This is a deep voice, a man.

"Shot. She's been shot. Right shoulder. Major blood loss."

At this point I hear sirens and another big van or truck. More boots.

People poking, prodding me, placing an oxygen mask over my nose and mouth. Sliding a stretcher under me. I levitate next. That part's cool . . . I've always wanted to be able to do that.

Evan's in my face again. "Insult me one more time, just so I know you're going to make it."

I try to come up with another bad word, but my brain doesn't cooperate. And then it sort of does—because I realize that for the first time ever, I want to say something *nice* to Evan Kincaid. This is totally shocking, but true.

"Let me have it, Kari."

I'm grinning under the oxygen mask.

"I can take it. C'mon."

With a superhuman effort, because they're so heavy, I manage to lift my left arm and hand and knock away the oxygen mask. "F-f—"

"Oooh. Now you're playing hardball," he says.

"*Friend,*" I announce.

For a moment there's dead silence.

Then Evan laughs, long and hard. "I think I'm going to faint."

One of the paramedics pushes the oxygen mask into place before I can say "Me too." And darkness closes in around me once again.

When I wake up, I'm in a hospital bed under clean sheets and blankets. There's an IV running into my hand and a weird clip on one of my fingers. My shoulder is killing me. And as I open my eyes, I see Evan and Charlie sprawled in blue vinyl chairs next to me. They've dozed off.

"Hey, guys," I whisper. "How're you doing?"

They bolt upright.

"Kari!" Charlie shouts. "You woke up! How are you feeling?"

"Like new," I lie.

"Does it hurt a lot?"

"Nah."

He jumps up and wriggles onto the bed with me.

"Easy," Evan warns him. "No matter what she says, she's in pain, and she's lost a lot of blood."

"Did you know that the human body contains about ten pints of blood?" Charlie asks. "And has *sixty-thousand miles* of arteries and veins? And two hundred and six bones?"

I shake my head.

"Know the difference between an artery and a vein?"

"Nope."

"An artery flows *from* the heart, and a vein flows *to* the heart."

"That's pretty cool, kiddo."

Charlie then explains to me, in proper medical jargon, how the surgeon removed the bullet from my shoulder and exactly what ligaments and tissues were damaged.

I catch Evan's amused gaze over Charlie's earnest, cowlicked head. *You gotta love this kid.*

"So, are you going to go to medical school?" Evan asks him.

I start to say that Mom and Dad would like that and almost bite my tongue off when I remember what's happened.

"Maybe," Charlie muses. "After I go to marine biology school and nuclear physicist school and maybe artificial intelligence school . . ."

Evan seems to note the darkening of my mood. "Hey, Brain Man, why don't we go get a soda? Your sister's still quite knackered—"

Charlie frowns. "What's that mean?"

"Tired."

"Oh."

"So we should let her rest."

"But I was going to explain how the process of anes-thesiology works—you know, what it does to the brain and all—"

"Later," Evan says firmly.

I smile my thanks to him.

He nods and takes Charlie by the hand and out the door. That's when I notice that there are two agents out-side, flanking it to keep an eye on us.

When Evan returns, I'm alarmed to see that he's alone.

"Charlie?" I croak.

"Your irrepressibly precocious little brother has suited up and scrubbed in as a guest in the OR," Evan informs me. "The surgeon who worked on you has allowed him to 'supervise' a similar procedure, though there's no bul-let involved in this one, thank God."

I start laughing, which hurts, so I stop immediately. I take a deep breath. "My parents?"

"Must have made their getaway clean. They took along Sophie and the microchip as well. While she's no big loss, the chip is a devastating one for the Agency."

"What was on it?" I'm almost afraid to ask.

He sighs. "Evidently it contained a complete list of all the KGB2 agents. It would have been utterly indispensable to the Agency, allowing them to roll up the entire network."

"KGB2?" *Please don't let this be what it sounds like.*

"It's a sort of neo-KGB, formed by a faction of the old one that never died." Evan yawns hugely, accentuating the air of exhaustion that hangs around him. His eyes are bloodshot, with huge purple circles underneath them. I wonder how long it's been since he truly slept.

"Kari," he says, "I'm not going to lie to you. The KGB2 is a particularly nasty bunch. And your parents have been mixed up with them from the get-go."

I avert my gaze from his. "I don't want to know this."

"I wouldn't either. But you can't hide from the truth."

Can too. I want very badly to do just that. But unfortunately, Evan is right.

"So what else is on the chip?" All this time I had a tiny bomb hanging from my wrist. Placed there by my own mom and dad. I could have been kidnapped for it or killed for it. In fact both things almost occurred. And they didn't give a damn that they put my life in danger.

"That chip also would have fully incriminated your parents," Evan says. "So they were desperate to get it."

"And now they've disappeared. Leaving me and Charlie to fend for ourselves."

Evan clears his throat and looks down at the floor. "Yes. I'm sorry."

I'm still trying to come to terms with it all. That my parents have lied to us, used us, betrayed us, and now abandoned us. It's beyond comprehension.

But there's more.

"So," I say, cutting my gaze toward the agents posted outside the door. "Will they let Charlie and me go home? Can we continue to live in our house and go to our schools?"

As soon as the words are out of my mouth, though, I know the answer.

There's real pain, real sympathy in Evan's eyes as he shakes his head.

"But I'm fully capable of taking care of Charlie!" My voice has risen at least two octaves, and my battered body begins to shake.

Evan takes my hand. "Kari, you're only sixteen."

"So? What's that got to do with anything?" I struggle to a sitting position, in spite of my shrieking shoulder. "I can cook. I can do laundry. I can go to his parent-teacher conferences. It will be *fine*."

"I don't know how to tell you this, but—"

"No. No! Not going to happen!" I shout at Evan.

"You and Charlie will have to go into foster care."

"Over my dead body. Absolutely not! I won't allow it." I'm starting to really freak out now. Charlie is not going into some strange household with people who might abuse him or assault him or worse.

"Calm down, Kari."

"I won't calm down!" I scream. "This isn't negotiable, Evan." I throw my legs over the side of the hospital bed and physically fight him when he tries to hold me flat on the mattress.

"Nurse!" he yells.

I rage, kick, and flail, even though I don't have an iota of my usual energy.

Evan finally lies flat on top of me, pinning me everywhere.

"Get off! Let me go!" I burst into tears that I shouldn't have the energy to produce. Still, I struggle. And I'm starting to hyperventilate.

"Nurse!" he shouts again. "Kari, please calm down. There's another option—"

But I barely hear him.

It's all too much: first my parents disappearing, then me being worried sick about them. Then trying to find them. Learning that Sophie is a psycho. Getting shot. Discovering that my own flesh and blood spies for Russia and has been lying to us, using us. Now they want to take Charlie away from me?

A nurse comes barreling in to the room, sees Evan on top of me, and probably jumps to the worst conclusion. "What is going on here? Get off her!"

"She needs sedation," Evan says.

"Off!"

He reluctantly complies.

I come screaming off the bed, jump to my feet, and promptly collapse. Blood loss and lack of oxygen and emotional trauma will do that to you. But I fight them as best I can as they pick me up and lay me back on the bed.

"You're not taking him! Not taking him! Not taking him!"

"Jesus, Joseph, and Mary," says the nurse. She calls for reinforcements.

Someone comes running in with a syringe full of something.

"No!" I yell. "No, no, no—"

But they plunge the needle into me anyway.

I will never forgive Evan for this.

Friend? Did I really call him *friend*?

Out of the corner of my eye I see him slam his fist into the wall and swear.

Within seconds my eyes roll back in my head, and I drop into unconsciousness once again.

Chapter Twenty-Three

When I return to the land of the living, the first thing I hear is Evan's voice—of course. He is my scourge. My nemesis.

"I made a complete hash out of it," he says into the cell phone at his ear. "I never even got to tell her the other part. She went ape-shit. Bonkers. Stark, staring mad."

There's a pause.

"Because of the concept of foster care for Charlie. Yes, she's sleeping now, but they had to sedate her. I'll tell her about the program when she wakes up."

"What program?" I ask coldly.

Evan whirls. "Gotta go," he says into the phone. "She's conscious. I'll ring you back." And he ends the call. "Kari!"

"You are scum," I say distinctly. "Where's my brother? Or have you already booked him into the foster-care system?"

"Kari, it isn't as if *I*, personally, decided your fates. It's U.S. law. So stop blaming me. Be quiet and *listen* to me this time. What I was trying to tell you—"

"I can't believe you pinned me down. I can't believe you let them sedate me. I can't believe—"

"Shut up!" Evan roars. "Or I'll do it again."

I stare at him disdainfully, resenting every lousy molecule of Kincaid permeating the room.

"What I was *trying* to tell you, before you went *mad*, is that you and Charlie don't have to go into foster care!"

I narrow my eyes at him. "What do you mean?"

"There's a program. It's the group that I'm a part of, actually. Called G.I."

I curl my lip. "Like G.I. Joe?"

"Something like that," Evan says. "It stands for Generation Interpol. Anyway, if you join, then you and Charlie can stay together and avoid foster care. But you have to decide now."

"Right now?"

"Yes, immediately."

"This is the special program you joined when you were thirteen?"

He nods. "And that was Agent Morrow I was just talking to on the phone."

"Are you happy in it?"

"I am. And let's be honest—I'd be in some reform school, if not for G.I. So what do you say?"

I frown. "Why do you have to have an answer this minute?"

"I'd tell you, but then I'd have to kill you," he jokes.

"Ha, ha." I glare moodily at him.

While I don't understand the time crunch, it's really not a hard decision, is it? Have Charlie taken away from me and be placed with strangers in foster care, or keep him with me and get trained as a junior Interpol agent.

"I'm in," I tell Evan. "On two conditions."

"Which are?"

"One: My friends, the ones who helped me break into Langley, are not charged or penalized by the government."

Evan nods. "I can't do anything about their parents' punishments, but I should be able to get the feds off their backs."

"Two: Charlie and I will have the right to take leave and hunt down our parents if we ever decide to do that—with the full support and resources of this G.I. program."

Evan gives me a long, hard stare. "That could be very dangerous."

"I don't care."

He shrugs. "All right then. Deal."

We shake on it. Then Evan calls Agent Morrow and says, "They're in." He ends the call and turns back to me. "Now, I suggest that you get some more sleep, little shrew."

"Yeah? Well I have a suggestion for you, too."

His lips twitch. "I'm sure you do."

"Glad we understand each other, Evan."

He winks at me. "I'll just sod off then, shall I?"

I point at the door. "You shall."

It's only later that I thank him for getting me and Charlie into the G.I. program. Evan Kincaid is not all bad. Just mostly.

I sleep for twenty-six hours straight, and when I wake up, Charlie is next to me in one of the vinyl chairs, still wearing the set of women's green scrubs that they gave him the day before when he "supervised" the other operation. They're huge on him, with the legs rolled up about five times.

His fingers are flying over the keyboard of a laptop.

"Morning, kiddo," I say, sleepily.

"It's afternoon," Charlie tells me, still clattering away. "Hey, you want to see a gall bladder operation?"

"Gee, let me think. No."

"But it's so cool . . . especially the part where they cut into the guy with the scalpel."

I shudder. "Not really my thing, Charlie Brown."

"Fine, but you're totally missing out."

"And I'm okay with that. Really."

"How's your shoulder?"

"Better," I lie. "Feels almost like new."

Charlie stops typing and pats his pocket. Something rattles. "I forgot to show you." He pulls out a plastic pill bottle and makes quick work of the "childproof" lid. He shakes an object into his hand and holds it up between his thumb and index finger.

It's a bullet.

"This is what they dug out of your shoulder," Charlie tells me.

I probably turn a little green. I feel green, anyway. "And you wanted it as a souvenir?"

Charlie nods. "The doc gave it to me."

I'm shaking my head at this when the doctor himself comes in. He's tall, thin, and bald with wire-rimmed glasses, bright blue eyes, and very white teeth. He high-fives Charlie.

"How's my best OR supervisor?"

"Good," Charlie says. "By the way, I'm going to recommend that you get promoted."

The doctor grins. "Well, thank you very much. That's generous of you."

"No," Charlie assures him. "It's entirely based on merit and skill."

The doc's lips twitch, and he nods, then turns to me. "Hello, young lady. I'm Dr. Travis. How are you feeling?"

I grimace. "Not quite ready to water-ski."

He laughs. "We'll get you there."

"Yeah."

Charlie drops the bullet back into the pill bottle and closes the lid.

"Thanks for entertaining my brother and giving him that grisly memento, by the way. He treasures it."

"My pleasure," the doc says, rocking back on his heels. He takes my chart and flips through it, looking at various vital signs. "Good, good. If everything continues to look like this, then there shouldn't be a problem discharging you and clearing you for travel tomorrow."

"Travel?"

"Yes. I understand from Mr. Kincaid that you're going to Paris. In confidence, of course."

This is definitely news to me. "Right," I say, looking to Charlie to see if he knows anything about this. He nods, his eyes bright.

"Hey, doc," my brother says. "Ask me how *I* feel."

"How do you feel, Charlie?" Dr. Travis asks, good-naturedly.

"Eiffel!" Charlie shrieks with laughter.

The doc and I groan.

Satisfied that his patient is recovering well, Dr. Travis leaves, promising to look in on me early tomorrow morning.

A nurse comes in and gives me antibiotics and a pain pill. I have a sudden craving for Peanut M&M's and beg Charlie to go get me some from a vending machine.

He does.

I've just opened the bag, popped three or four into my mouth, and crunched down when Evan ushers in Luke, Lacey, Rita, and Kale.

"Luke!" I can't stop myself from beaming a huge smile at him. "Rita! Kale! Lacey. I can't believe you're all here. . . ."

"Oh. My. God." Lacey says, staring at my mouth. "That is disgusting."

"Seen a dentist lately, love?" Evan inquires with a wink.

Luke bursts out laughing as I cover my mouth in horror. Then, to my shock, he walks up and kisses me—right on the mouth. Chocolate and nuts and everything.

Charlie whoops.

Lacey covers her eyes. "Oh, barf."

"I'm so glad you're okay," Luke says, setting a big

bouquet of flowers on the nightstand, then taking my hand and squeezing it.

Luke Carson just kissed me! Voluntarily. And he's holding my hand! I'm going to die. Explode with happiness. If all I had to do was get shot in the shoulder for this to happen, I'm ready to sacrifice my other one too.

I know that there are three other friends here to see me, but I can't seem to look away from Luke. He's wearing jeans and a forest-green shirt that defines the muscles in his arms and shoulders and brings out the color of his eyes. The hand that's holding mine is warm and strong, and I want him to never let go.

"Completely unfair," remarks Evan, to nobody in particular. "I kiss her—just to hide her face from potential bad guys, mind you—and I get kicked into a wall for my trouble. *Luke* kisses her, and she clings to him like a koala to a eucalyptus tree."

My face heats up, and Luke turns red too. "Yeah, I heard about that." He levels his gaze on Evan, as if to warn him not to do it again.

I seriously think my heart is going to explode. Someone can shoot me in the left butt cheek, and then I'll present the right one, if only Luke will be my boyfriend.

"I figure I was taking my life in my hands by planting one on you," he teases me. "But I've wanted to do that for a really long time, Kari."

"Y-you have?" I squeak.

"Yep. But I thought you were dating that guy." He jerks a thumb at Kale.

"Oh. No." I blink, hard, as I notice that Kale and Rita

are holding hands. "Uh . . . am I seeing things or—"

"The brat decided to try slumming with me for a while," Kale says, grinning.

"The truth is that I felt sorry for the grease monkey," retorts Rita.

He pulls her close to him, slides his hand down, and pinches her on the bottom.

"Hey!" she squeals, and hits him with a huge purple teddy bear that she's evidently brought for me.

"What did I tell you?" Evan says, shaking his head. "They were hot for each other."

Kale's brought me balloons that he ties to the rolling tray the staff puts my meals on. Rita sets the bear on the end of the bed, and I laugh at its goofy expression. Someone glued one of its eyes higher than the other, and it has a little pink tongue that hangs out the side of its mouth.

"I couldn't find a Kung Fu Panda," she says. "But I thought this bear was cute."

"Definitely," I agree. "Thanks."

Kale shoves his hands into his pockets and shakes his head at me. "Mighty Mouse," he says. "I know you're a big hero, but did you have to jump in front of that bullet?"

"Guess so."

"You are all such dorks." Lacey elbows him out of the way, steps forward, and gives me a wrapped gift.

I'm taken aback. "Thank you."

"Well, aren't you going to open it?"

Obediently I tear off the wrapping paper. She's given me one of those all-in-one travel makeup kits, a nice one. It's Estee Lauder. I wonder where she stole it?

"Just for the record," Lacey declares, "I didn't buy it with the five-fingered discount."

"Lacey, this is so sweet of you."

She tosses her hair and hands me an envelope. "Don't even try to use it until you read my instructions and look carefully at the diagrams."

Rita cackles.

"Say," asks Evan. "Does that have eyeliner and mascara in it?"

"Shut up, Evan." I glare at him.

"I'm out," Lacey says. "But I understand that you're going on a trip, so I wanted to say good-bye and good luck. And that you have my permission to date my stinky brother if you really want to—but only from a distance."

Luke's face and neck flush bright red. "Thanks, Lace. Appreciate that."

My face feels like it's on fire.

"But you still owe me that two hundred bucks," she says as a parting shot. She gives a little beauty-queen wave as she exits my hospital room. "Don't forget!"

Everyone laughs. But I realize that I have no idea where my backpack has gone . . . with all that cash in it.

"Evan?" I query. "Is this G.I. thing a paid gig?"

He nods.

"Oh, good. I wasn't sure how many French kids I'd have to babysit to make two hundred dollars. And I wouldn't even be able to understand them."

"I'll take care of my sister," Luke says. "You don't owe her anything. Besides, this is her only outing for a very long time. The two of us are grounded for life plus twenty years."

Oh, ouch. "I'm so sorry that I got you into all of this . . . are you all in big trouble with your parents?"

Kale shrugs. "No martial arts classes or tournaments for a whole year."

I sigh. That's going to devastate him, no matter how casual he's acting about it.

My gaze shifts to Rita. "You?"

Rita grimaces. "I'm forbidden to use any kind of technology for six months. No laptop, no cell phone, no iPad . . . I'm going to go nuts!"

I gape at her. "How are you going to write papers?"

"On an AlphaSmart." She pronounces it as if it's a dirty word. "My parents are pissed off with a capital *PO*, especially because I embarrassed Senator Dad professionally." She tosses her ponytail and rolls her eyes behind the red Prada glasses she has on.

"It turns out that when you try to hack into the Agency director's laptop? Well, 'Backtrack' trips security—and then the Agency watches your every move. They must have been laughing at us the entire time. They *let* us walk in there. That security guard, Jake? He knew the minute Lacey took his badge. They just played along."

"Kinda sucked for the agents who got beat up, though," Kale says, with a smirk.

I grimace as I think of Mitch. "Some of them deserved it."

"Hazards of the job," Evan muses. "And actually, they were quite impressed with us—especially you, Kari, regarding your unusual skill set and having the nerve to break into Langley. The Agency is actually a little pissed that Interpol is taking you, but they don't have a similar training program for kids, so their hands are tied."

Evan looks around at my friends. "Speaking of Interpol, I'll have to ask you to say your good-byes now. Kari's got to rest, as we leave tomorrow. She'll be in training almost immediately, fractured shoulder or not. G.I. students have to be at the top of their game, always."

Rita and Kale hug me.

"Got Skype?" Luke asks.

I look at Evan.

"We've got everything," he says. "You'll even be able to do a virtual snog, if you must."

Luke looks puzzled.

"Kiss," Evan says, in irritated tones. "Make out. Suck face. Whatever you Yanks call it. Bloody hell, do I have to translate everything?" He walks to the door.

Luke comes and sits next to me on the bed. "I think the real thing is better," he says, softly. "Don't you?"

And then he lowers his head to mine, covers my mouth with his, and kisses me like he really means it. I almost pass out.

"Christ, aren't you done yet?" Evan calls over his shoulder as he slouches against the doorway.

"Not nearly," Luke murmurs against my lips.

Finally he raises his head and cups my face in his hands. "But to tell you the truth, I kind of miss those M&M's."

Chapter Twenty-Four

Evan grants one last request before we leave for Paris and G.I. He drives Charlie and me to our house to get some of our things and promises that the place will be well taken care of by a property management agency.

I look at our home through different eyes now. The old red bricks look to me like lies, piled one on top of the other. The black door seems ominous. And the fake red impatiens in the window boxes speak for themselves: Nothing was ever real around here.

Mr. Carson has released some very disturbing information to me over the past few hours. I was probably an accident that forced my parents to get married. And Mom's old e-mails show that she deliberately set out to have Charlie because her KGB2 bosses wanted her to get into the analyst's side of the Agency. They even gave her money toward in vitro fertilization, believe it or not.

It's so wrong, so awful, so inhuman that Charlie came into being this way—not as a baby who was wanted and loved, but as a tool for duplicity and crime and betrayal.

And he's such a little miracle, my brother.

One thing is for sure, I will never, ever tell him how he came to be born or why. It would be cruel, and it doesn't matter now. He's adorable and brilliant and loving and loyal—to me, and to his country.

We go inside the house, and I find myself shaking with anger and revulsion. I want to knock all the beautiful things off the walls and smash them. Each item represents a stretch of weeks that Mom and Dad neglected me and Charlie for some mission in a faraway place.

It's one thing to leave your kids in order to serve your country. It's another to leave your kids so that you can steal and smuggle information to people who are their sworn enemies.

Oh—and use your children to do it.

My charm bracelet tinkles on my wrist as I push the door closed behind us, and I'm seized with a pathological need to get it off my body, away from my skin. I yank on it until one of the links breaks, and I walk it into the kitchen, Evan and Charlie following curiously behind.

"Kari, what are you doing?" Charlie asks.

In answer, I walk straight to the kitchen sink and turn on the water, then the garbage disposal. I tear one charm at a time off the bracelet and drop it down the black rubber hole, listening as the steel teeth chew up the soft silver.

First goes the Roman Colosseum.

Then the little Spanish bull.

Followed by the Greek Venus de Milo. And so on.

"You could be disposing of evidence," Evan says. "Pun intended."

I shake my head. "No. These are just the copies. Sophie took the real ones, and the Agency has quite a few of them, as you know. If they'd wanted these, they'd have taken the bracelet from me before now."

The last charm—Bran Castle—falls into the black hole and makes a particularly horrible noise as it gets ground up. I guess that's fitting as the grand finale—I drop the chain in after it, and the noise gets worse.

"You're hell in the kitchen, aren't you?" Evan observes.

I look around, inhaling the familiar smells that years of cooking have left in this room. My mom's made count-less dinners for the family in here. I wonder if each one of them was made with bitterness and resentment?

But the funny thing is that even now, I know that's not true. My mom truly enjoyed being a mom. And my dad liked being a dad.

I don't think you can fake that stuff. Maybe it's possible for a few days, or a week. But not day in, day out, for six-teen years.

I see Mom's tears as our parents walked out the door. I remember that defeated, exhausted expression of Dad's. And I think of Charlie's last birthday, when Dad stayed up most of the night putting together this robotic creature for him. (Charlie, of course, immediately dismantled it and rebuilt it so that he could see how it worked.) Mom and I baked his rocket-shaped cake and had so much fun decorating it . . . in red, white, and blue. She wasn't faking that joy. Dad wasn't faking his dedication to his son.

Were they?

I become angry all over again—because they've thrown everything away. They've thrown away the love, the memories, the family itself. And for that, I'll never forgive them.

This kitchen, with its history of good times, is now the saddest place imaginable. I shut off the disposal and the water and wipe my hands on my jeans. Then I turn on my heels and walk out. We've got to get moving.

We stop in Charlie's room next, with it's theme of outer space. We pack a few of his clothes—in particular, he wants an old red sweatshirt and his favorite jeans. We throw in khakis and shirts and underwear and socks and a jacket. We take the Snoopy stuffed animal that he's had since he was a tiny baby. He wants to take books, but they're too bulky. I promise him that we'll get him an e-reader. He makes me swear that we'll download a copy of *Roget's Thesaurus* on it.

His gaze goes to the robot in the corner. He walks over and kicks it.

Then we go to my room. I remember painting the walls purple with my mom and squeeze my eyes shut. I remember how my dad, though he hated the idea, painted all the trim in the room a high-gloss black. Purple walls and black trim made the room dark, but I loved it. Now I never want to see those colors again.

I yank a duffle out of my closet and throw in some basics. I carefully fold my *gi* and add that, along with my proudly earned brown belt. I toss in my iPad and its cord, though I guess I'll have to get some kind of adapter in Paris.

Finally, I take a framed picture of me and Kale in a karate competition, one of me and Rita, and one of me and Charlie. I lay the photos that have my parents in them face down on the dresser.

Evan sticks his head through the doorway. "Ready?"

I take a deep breath. "Not quite."

I get logs from the woodpile. I grab some old newspaper from the garage. And a box of long matches.

Charlie and Evan follow me out to the backyard, where I dump everything by the old fire pit that Dad constructed years ago. There are memories here, too, of singing campfire songs, huddling in blankets, and telling ghost stories.

Ten minutes later Charlie and Evan and I stand around a small bonfire.

"I didn't know you were a pyromaniac in addition to all of your other talents," Evan says. "What is it that you want to burn?"

"Hey, can we make s'mores?" Charlie asks.

I think of Sophie and the special version of s'mores she invented for my little brother. Sophie, whom our parents brought into our lives. That makes me coldly furious all over again. "No, kiddo. Not today."

I walk into the house and make my way to the living room. I march up to the fireplace and yank the family portrait off its hook. Dad and Mom and the then-clueless me and Charlie smile up into my face: two big fat lies and the kids who now hate them.

I wrestle the painting out back. I hold it over the fire.

"Hey," Evan tells me. "There's an envelope with your name on it taped to the back of the picture."

"I don't care," I say.

"What if there's a letter from your parents in there? Cash?"

I shrug. "Charlie, do you have a problem with me doing this?"

He looks at the painting, at our falsely happy, "all-American" family. At Mom and Dad with their hands on our shoulders, smiling for the artist.

He shakes his head.

I drop the painting facedown into the flames, and my brother slips his hand into mine as we watch it blacken, curl, and smoke.

Evan stands somberly for a moment with his hands in his pockets. Then he reaches down and snatches the envelope before it can burn. "Shall I open it?"

"I don't care," I tell him stonily. "If you do, then open it in private and keep whatever's in there to yourself."

We stay there until there's nothing left but a few shreds. Then we shovel ashes over them and make triply sure there are no burning embers.

Evan puts one arm around Charlie's shoulders and the other around mine as we walk out of the back garden gate for the last time. We get into his car without saying a word and drive away from our home, from our lives, from everything we once took blissfully for granted.

I hope we're ready for Generation Interpol.

And I hope Generation Interpol is ready for *us*.